USA *Today* Bestselling Author
Dale Mayer

TERKEL'S TEAM SERIES
TERK'S TRIUMPH
BOOK 09

TERKEL'S TRIUMPH: TERKEL'S TEAM, BOOK 9
Beverly Dale Mayer
Valley Publishing Ltd.

ISBN-13: 978-1-773365-33-6
Print Edition

Books in This Series:

About This Book

Welcome to a brand-new series from *USA Today* best-selling author Dale Mayer, where dark-ops SEALs have special senses and skills, needed to solve intrigue, betrayal, and ... murder. A series with all the elements you've come to love, plus so much more, ... including psychics!

The move to a castle is both daunting and exhilarating. Damn sure he has bitten of more than he can handle, Terk asks Charles for help. In turn, Charles brings in an old friend to get the team installed and to get the castle renovated and organized. Going into private business never looked so good or so hard. But, with Levi and Ice joining in the fun, even Bullard helping out, the renovations are in Emmaline's capable hands, and all is well.

Or is it? When Jonas calls to say there's a problem, and it's heading their way, Terk knows the priority is safety and security. But what does that look like with a large group of energy workers? There's also another side effect of so much energy all in one place—something no one thought about—and something that's way too late to stop ...

Sign up to be notified of all Dale's releases here!
https://geni.us/DaleNews

PROLOGUE

ALMOST ONE MONTH later, as they landed in London, Celia winced because her lower back and the long flight had not been a good combination.

"You and the babies okay?" Terk murmured as he ushered her toward the big SUV waiting for them.

"Yep." She yawned heavily. "They're both more than ready to rest though, and so am I."

"Lots of rest coming up,"

"We still don't have a home yet," she said, looking at him.

"Depends on how you feel about being part of a big compound."

"Like Ice and Levi's?"

He chuckled. "Yeah. Something like that."

As they drove out of town, she thought about a compound and what that would be like as a home, a working home. But when the drive went a little longer than expected, she turned and asked, "Where are we going?"

"Charles suggested a new place as a base. I've been there before, but I didn't realize it was up for sale."

"What kind of a place is it?"

He looked over at her, as they started to climb a mountain. "How do you feel about something fairly old-fashioned?"

She frowned. "As long as it's got all the modern amenities—inside plumbing, hot water, electricity, and communications—I don't hate the idea, especially if it's got some history and charm."

He laughed, as they entered through a huge stone wall and a double gate.

She looked at him in shock. "Oh my God. Is this a castle?"

"Kind of." Terk chuckled. "It looks like it might be big enough for the expanding family."

"What is there, like twenty of us or something?" she asked.

"So far, nineteen, counting our twins. Plus, we'll need people to help run the place, like weapons specialists, builders, tech support, culinary staff, housekeeping, gardeners, and whatever else. We'll need a bunch of staff, unless you've got a problem with that."

She stared at the unfolding landscape, as they drove around and came into full view of the castle, and she was just stunned. "Is that a moat?" she cried out in delight, as the grassy grounds went straight to the water's edge. She bounced out of the SUV and raced over to the water in an awkwardly pregnant hop.

"I see you approve of it, but I don't think the twins appreciate the bouncing."

She laughed, holding her belly. "Is there a pool too?"

"There is a pool. Now, we haven't finalized any of the legal arrangements yet, but the plan is to spend a few days here, while we think about it."

"What's to think about?" she cried out, turning to look at him in shock. "Sign on the dotted line. I think it's perfect."

He had to admit that he thought so too. As he looked around at the grounds, he could envision them all here.

She whispered, "Can we really afford this?"

"We can afford it, especially since the US government has paid for it," he said, chuckling.

"Considering that they tried to kill us all, and we could have had them caught up in litigation for decades and would have gotten the money anyway," she murmured, "it's pretty much all good."

"Exactly, so, in theory, we've just saved them money." He reached out for her hand. "Come on. Let's go take a look at our new home."

Just then the front door opened, and an older man leaned against the door, a gentle smile on his face.

"Charles?" Terk said in delight. "I wasn't expecting to see you here."

He nodded, beaming at Terk and Celia. "Not sure how you feel about it, but I thought I'd meet you here and make sure everything was in order."

The men shook hands, and Terk introduced Celia to Charles. She was immediately drawn to the charming older man. "It's very nice to meet you, and I hope you'll stay." She was filled with joy, as she reached out and hugged him, already enjoying the kind energy of this man.

Charles flushed with pleasure. "How sweet of you. I do have a friend here with me." Celia watched as an older woman walked—with an obvious limp—toward them along the long central hallway.

As the men stepped away to look at something on the property, the woman approached Celia and smiled, holding out her hand. "Hello, I am Emmeline. Charles and I are old school friends."

"So nice to meet you. I'm Celia." She couldn't take her eyes off the woman, immediately noting that Emmeline was the type who only grew more beautiful with age.

"This is such a beautiful and peaceful place. I already want to visit again," Emmeline replied.

"Absolutely." Celia hugged the woman. She looked over at Terk, as he and Charles returned. "I don't think anybody here will mind, and the place looks to be huge. I hope we can get it."

"Oh, wait until you see inside it," Emmaline said. "It's amazing."

"Perfect." Celia beamed. "All I want to do now is explore, and then I want to hit that pool, wherever it is."

Charles laughed. "It's being uncovered right now. It should be ready within the hour, so probably about the time the tour is complete," he said affectionately. "I also took the liberty of having a meal prepared."

Celia grinned at him. "I knew I liked you already." She reached out to grab Terk's hand. "Come on, Terk. Our future is waiting." *The pool is also waiting for us,* she whispered in his mind.

What about the twins?

They can handle it. So can we.

CHAPTER 1

D R. PHILLY "CELIA" Waterball walked down to the end of the hallway and stared out one of the huge arched windows. Terk's energy drifting toward her; just moments later she felt Terk's hands on her shoulders.

"Are you okay?" he murmured against her ear.

She leaned into him. "Better than okay." She sighed. "This is definitely not where I expected to end up."

"As long as you're okay with this as a destination."

"It would be awfully hard to change it now." She laughed.

"This would be the time to change it though. The paperwork is just now going through."

"So how is it we're living here already then?"

"Because we rented it for a little while to ensure we'll be okay here. But the paperwork was submitted, based on our intent to purchase."

"Got it. And, yes, I'm totally okay to stay here."

"You won't miss London?"

"If I do, it's a quick hop away—and the same for the US, though a much longer trip. I really like your friends over there. ... And family too," she added, as an afterthought.

Terk chuckled. "Merk is likely to spend a fair bit of time over here too. We've always been close. Our paths diverged in the military, but it's never been our intent to be separated."

"No, I'm sure you didn't." She stared out at the massive fields surrounding the castle. "What is here, ten acres or something?"

"Closer to twenty-five. I can pull out the specs, if you want to know for sure."

"No." She shook her head. "That's not necessary. I just can't imagine even having something like this. It seems so vast and yet so perfect."

He laughed. "You look at it from the picturesque point of view," he said affectionately. "And I'm looking at it from the standpoint of defense, secrecy, privacy, and all those good things."

"Of course you are," she murmured. "And you always will."

He nodded. "I think at this point, it's pretty well ingrained in us."

"Is the whole team okay to live here?"

"Yeah, though, as soon as we can, we'll seek out opportunities to expand our holdings into neighboring areas, so that we have a continuous supply for expansion," he murmured.

She twisted to look up at him. "Seriously?"

He nodded. "It's never a good idea to have everybody in one location. That's just a standard defense tactic. However, it's definitely important that everybody still have the same access to security. So, as we expand to the neighboring properties, we'll add tunnel systems and security between each of the properties."

"Wow, that is more elaborate than I expected. Does everybody on the team really want to set up a new company?"

Terk nodded again. "I think everybody realizes we're

uniquely prepared for this, and who else understands us except for the rest of the team? Plus, the rest of the world doesn't really care or even know we exist."

"No, I'm sure they don't. Although, in fairness, how could they? This is just so far beyond what is normal."

"Yet it's definitely normal for us and for you." He tapped gently on her chin. "Remember?"

She chuckled. "Never in my wildest dreams did I think this was ever possible."

"Sometimes you've got to let dreams just happen on their own. Don't try to manufacture anything. Just sit back, and let it happen."

"And I love that theory, but, after my divorce and years of thinking I would always be alone, and alone with my abilities as well"—she shook her head—"it's hard to see how it's even possible."

"Ah, that's okay. Just leave it to us. We'll get you where you want to be."

"I'm already exactly where I want to be," she murmured, linking her arms around his, as they wrapped around her belly from behind. "There's just so much to be done, even to get set up."

"That's why I'm wondering if you want to go some-where else, until the birth, so you're not part of all this chaos."

"No, I'm fine." She smiled. "And I know you're just try-ing to protect me, but I don't think there's any more danger, is there?"

"Would like to think not. I mean, obviously an awful lot still needs to be dealt with on many levels, but we're on it. Yet, because so many different elements were involved in trying to eliminate my team, I'm not sure I can ever be 100 percent positive."

"That'll always bother you, won't it?"

He nodded calmly. "Sure it will, as it'll be something that I'll always keep in mind and look for opportunities to do something about."

"You keep it in mind, but don't worry because we're just fine." She patted her belly again.

"Good, still there's been no progress on tracking down whether or not there are other eggs."

"God, I hope not," she murmured.

"It'll be something we may never get final answers on," he added cautiously.

She realized just how much that bothered him and that he was afraid it would bother her as well. She nodded slowly. "I get that, and I think we have no choice but to go on faith that, if more show up, we'll deal with it then."

He kissed the top of her head. "I sure as heck wasn't expecting this problem."

"Neither was I. Imagine how I felt." She gave a nervous laugh.

"I can't even begin to imagine that. It must have been a frightening shock."

"Absolutely, but a lot of good came from all this, so it's hard to get too angry."

"That's a hell of a reason for finding forgiveness."

"Sometimes we must forgive because anything else would drive us too crazy. Forgiveness is not for them. It's for us."

"Agreed," he murmured, "and you're a very smart cookie."

She chuckled at that. "I don't know about the smart cookie remark. I'm just somebody who loves you."

"And I love you."

They stood in a sweet silence for several moments, and then he said, "Anytime you want to go lie down, we do have some more furniture moved in. And we have multiple trucks coming over the next few days."

She chuckled. "Yeah, things are a little sparse at the moment, and that's fine. I'm not breakable."

"You *are* breakable but hopefully not that breakable."

"I'm perfectly okay to rest on what we have."

"That's good, and I know Charles is hiring us some staff."

"Have you considered trying to get Charles to stay?"

"I think he probably will stay close by, but I don't think he wants to live on the compound."

"Is there a particular reason for that?"

"I'm not sure if there is or not," Terk murmured, "except we have an awful lot of people in our growing team. He's getting older, and I think he's just used to having his own space. Plus, he has an agreement with MI6, and I don't think he wants anything to jeopardize that or his own work."

"I can understand that too," she noted. "He is a lovely man."

"He is." Terk chuckled. "I don't think he'd have a problem being a godfather."

She smiled. "I already told him that our kids have no living grandparents, so we needed somebody nearby. I think he was tickled pink."

"I can tell you, without a doubt, that he was definitely tickled pink. He has a granddaughter he loves dearly but, so far, no great-grandkids." Terkel hugged her gently. "Many of us have availed ourselves of his skills and abilities and connections over the years," he shared. "Charles is a guy who tends to pop up in situations when you least expect it. Levi's team has been over here many times as well."

"Can I assume that, over time, I'll get to meet all these people?"

"Absolutely. You'll probably spend more time with them than you ever wanted."

"Right," she said, "but one of the first things we need is kitchen staff because there'll be a lot of people to feed here."

"I think Mariana wants domain over that."

"And I'm totally okay giving it to her, but she will need lots of help. And, if I could have a room for my research and lab work, then that would make me happy too."

He chuckled. "There are lot of rooms in this place."

"And I can see that. However, by the time you have it all planned out—with an armory, a weight room, a control room, a panic room, and all that defense-related allotment, not to mention the living quarters, there won't be as much extra space as I thought." She hesitated and then asked, "Will we also have a jail?"

He stiffened ever-so-slightly and then nodded. "Yeah. We really have to, just from a safety point of view."

"Fine," she said, with a heavy sigh.

"On that note," he murmured, "Levi and the team are coming over to help us get things set up."

"Oh, wow. That's really nice of them."

"It's what we do. I heard rumblings that Bullard may even come at some point."

She shook her head. "Aren't you all competing for the same business though?"

"No," he said, "we're all in complementary businesses, and each of us has our own skill sets and specialties. And let's face it. Some of our skills are ones that we learned from each other."

"Ah," she murmured. "So, in a way, they could also be people who would want your skills."

"Absolutely. Even if they don't necessarily know it yet." He chuckled.

"*Business*," she remarked, with a smile and a shake of her head. "I love it."

"Good, because there will be a lot of business going on here."

"I really like that whole big conference room yet dining room scenario that Ice has going. It was family-friendly, yet still worked from a business perspective."

"It does, and I like that too," Terk agreed. "We'll figure out something similar. I'm just not sure how to make it happen here."

"That," she said, with a laugh, "is because this place is *huge*."

"It is, but we'll get there. Everybody seems to be pretty excited about it. The electronic security equipment and battery backups, and even solar panels as a further backup, have been ordered. A start, at least. As soon as we can get everything connected and online, I know things will feel better."

"It's funny. That's one of the last things I'm worried about," she murmured.

"I'm surprised, what with your research and interest in energy workers. Maybe you are nesting, as the literature speaks of, in the last trimester, readying for the twins. The rest of us will get it set up, as everybody's work is dependent on being connected and able to communicate and access data globally. We feel a certain amount of anxiety, until everything is back up and running again."

She nodded. "Yeah, that makes sense. I also need to find a doctor and take care of a few things baby-wise. I haven't been for a medical checkup yet, beyond what Ice did at the compound. I probably should see an obstetrician."

"That's not a bad idea, if that's what you want to do," he murmured.

She looked up at him. "And I figured you'd expect me to go."

"I'm totally out of my element here. I only know what little I've read online and will trust that you know what you need to do. I'm completely in the dark when it comes to pregnancy and delivery."

"You and me both. But just to make sure we've got somebody to call on in case there's ever a problem, I figured I should probably find someone local."

"Anytime you want to go into town or to visit some-body," he said, "let me know, and I'll make sure we have a driver for you."

"And if it's to do with the pregnancy, will you come?" she asked, a note of challenge in her voice. Yet even as she said it, she was unsure why she was even testing him.

"If it's something you want me to attend, then I'll come," he stated. "If you'll just test out a doctor to see if you feel comfortable with him or her, I'm okay with leaving that up to you. Anytime you want me with you, then I'll come with you. However, I trust your intuition. Anytime you want my support, then I'm there." He gave her a gentle hug, soon hearing raised voices downstairs. "I'd better go see what's going on." And, with that, he dropped a kiss on her temple and let his hands fall away, as he headed to the stairs.

She turned around to watch as he disappeared, wondering if she should follow.

"One of the things I'd like to see maybe down the road," she muttered, "is an elevator." It would be good for her to keep using the stairs while she was pregnant. However, as she got further along, it would be kind of a pain to go up and down all these stairs all the time. And this castle had what? Four stories aboveground? And the ground floor itself seemed to be twenty feet tall. She hoped all the other floors weren't like that but wasn't sure, as she hadn't made her way to the top floor yet. As a matter of fact, she hadn't made her way very far at all, either inside the castle or out on the property itself, and so much was out there yet to explore. She turned to head to her room, contemplating maybe a nap or at least doing some research, then realized—until communication systems were connected—she was in the same boat as everybody else, and she would have to wait to get information.

Her phone rang just then, and she looked down to check her Caller ID. "Hello, Ice," she said cheerfully. "How are things in your corner of the world?"

"My corner is not bad," she said, with a smile in her voice. "How about yours?"

"Chaos," she replied. "Absolute chaos, but that's okay. We're making progress."

"I'm glad to hear that. Are you getting furniture and all that yet?"

"I think, from the sounds of things down below, a big truck may have just arrived."

"That's good news. I was calling, wondering if you were looking for somebody to take care of the housework over there."

"Yes, but I have no idea what that'll look like just yet, especially given Terk's focus on security."

"Okay, I talked to Charles about it, and I've given him a few names of vetted local folks."

"Oh, we'll need more than a little bit of help. I know Mariana wants to run the kitchen, but we need to hire some help for her too."

"If she's half as good a cook as they all say she is, then you're better off to leave that with her. I don't know what I'd do without Alfred and Bailey."

"I'm happy to have Mariana take that on," Celia stated, chuckling. "That is definitely not my domain. I don't mind managing the rest of house or the finances, but I wouldn't have a clue how to cook for a group like this."

"What you were versus what you'll become will redefine everything really. Once those kids start rolling through your world, things will change quickly." At that, Ice burst out laughing. "You're going to have so much fun."

"Honestly, it's been a pretty huge change already, without any of that."

"And it will just keep right on changing too," Ice noted, and together the two women shared a laugh and a story or two. Then Ice said, "I'll let you go, Celia. I just wanted to check in with you to make sure you're doing okay over there."

"It's all good." She still had a smile on her face when she hung up. Ice was just that kind of a person. Always concerned, always there to help. And Celia really appreciated it. They'd become close in the time that she'd stayed with her on the Houston compound, had grown closer after some of the mysteries of the attack on Terk's team and Celia had been unraveled, and since then, Ice and Celia had become good friends.

Who would have known that was something Celia

would ever crave? She hadn't had a whole lot of female companionship over the years, and it wasn't something that she'd ever thought of as a loss. However, now she realized what a loss it really was and looked forward to making friends with some of the women here.

Celia wasn't even sure how it would work herself, even with her energy working skills, but she was more than willing to do whatever they needed to make it happen. No doubt that some adjustments would be needed, because some people had abilities that gave them extra access to thought processes, and that was something they would try and set some ground rules for.

Celia couldn't believe that she was even thinking about things like that, but, as it crossed her mind, she realized she was probably the best person to sit down and to do that. So, with her laptop in hand, she headed over to the room she and Terk were currently occupying. A small table was at the far end, and she sat down there and started writing out a preliminary list. If nothing else, it would be important for the sake of everybody's sanity for them all to know how to navigate the uncharted waters of this living-together scenario, especially with all these advanced energy workers.

Establishing boundaries, so each person knew the lines they could and could not cross, would be a challenge in itself, because everybody's abilities here were quite new and still evolving. Thus some had no idea what they were supposed to do yet. And, as their abilities continued to grow and change in the future, the boundaries would need to be fluid as well.

It was very exciting and different, and Celia found herself really looking forward to making it work. She hadn't even imagined that something like this was possible, but she felt like she was here among friends and with people who were more like her than anyone else she'd ever been around. And that, in itself, was worth so much.

It was also pretty odd to think that so many people had these special abilities, although she had hunted high and low to find anybody. Kind of like Terk had himself, although he clearly had been more successful. Whoever would have thought that she would stumble into a dozen, if not more, already? And, as she knew from her own research, these numbers would just increase, as everybody started to learn to do more. Their energy would attract more people of the same ilk, as they continued to develop themselves. It was an exciting time, and Celia couldn't be happier.

And, with that, she bent down to her list once again.

AS TERK WALKED into the massive open area—what looked like the original medieval living room, with a hearth for the fireplace in the front—the space was currently filled with boxes. Several of Terk's team walked toward him, big grins on their faces. "Now what?" Terk asked, with an eye roll.

"Oh, that was nothing." Wade chuckled. "We're just never sure whether we're supposed to disturb you or not."

"The answer would be *not*," he said a little testily, but he knew that this was all in good fun. They were just getting used to everybody having partners right now, and the teasing was getting a little out of hand. It would have been one thing if it were just one at a time, but suddenly it was everyone, and it would take a little bit of time to work through it. Not to mention that these men on his original team were all still recovering to some degree.

"How is Mariana doing in the kitchen?" Terk asked.

"She's in her element," Calum said, adding a word of warning, "however, the existing main kitchen needs a lot of work, and she won't want to go too cheap. She found the servants' kitchen too and was excited to have a backup. Also she has several smaller businesses to run. so she needs help on one side or the other."

"The problem would be making sure she goes big enough in the main kitchen," Damon said. "And we'll have to get a lot of domestic and professional help. Terk, you know that, right?"

"Oh, I know." Terk nodded. "Levi and Ice got to start off small and grow into their team and compound setup. However, we're starting out with a bang, but at least we have their model and lessons learned to build from."

"And we can do it." Charles walked toward them, wearing a broad smile. "Ice has sent over some names of people you may want to consider bringing on board to give you a hand with the household."

"Cool, and Levi should be here soon." Terk looked down at his watch, frowned, and, as if on cue, his phone rang. "Hey, Levi. Where are you?" Terk put it on Speaker.

"We just landed," he said. "We're picking up the vehicle. Do you guys need anything?"

"Tons," Terk said cheerfully, "but there'll be more than a few rounds of supplies happening, either delivered or rounded up ourselves, so just come on over, and we'll put you to work."

"Good enough. We'll be there as soon as we can."

With that, Terk hung up, then looked over at the others. "So that'll give us a couple extra hands."

"How many are coming?" Damon asked curiously.

"Just my brother and Levi, as far as I know," Terk noted, "but I wouldn't be at all surprised if somebody else showed up."

At that, they all nodded, and Damon said, "We'll find out soon enough." He wandered with them down toward the far end of the huge front room.

"What would be nice," Terk said, "is if we could get some organization as to room assignments. Has anybody had a chance to check out the castle enough to make suggestions?"

"Yeah." Wade nodded. "We've been looking at that and have a good start on an inventory of the rooms."

Gage spoke up. "So far, we've worked out where we should have an armory, the jail, and some obvious choices for some storage. Plus, there's a huge walk-in freezer area downstairs. That could be very helpful."

"We also have access to outside that's connected to a farm area, including horse barns with stalls, feed storage, tack rooms, and things like that," Wade said. "This place just goes on and on. Outside and inside both." He shook his head. "There's got to be like two hundred rooms here."

"Which we'll need damn quickly." Terk frowned. "So let's finish up a solid inventory of everything in this building, including sizes, features, what floor they're on, and see what we can start assigning out, so we know what we need to get in for each of them. We'll also have to decide how much temporary help we want to bring in or if we want to keep most of this to ourselves for now."

"I don't think we can," Wade said. "We'll need a lot of help to get this initial setup done."

"That's what I was afraid of," Terk murmured. "Okay, so we need to get as much done as we can ourselves, particularly as long as Levi and his team are here, to at least get things sorted and organized. We might have to bring in some IT people."

"Or not." Damon frowned. "Only Stone, Levi, Ice, or Bullard can help us. Otherwise it opens us up to security breaches."

"Who helped Levi with their kickass system?"

"Bullard did," Damon murmured. "He's also dealing with a very pregnant wife right now."

"Jesus, that sure seems to be in the air," Wade said, grinning.

"It absolutely is in the air." Charles smiled. "Now I do have connections to help get you guys set up, and, as I mentioned, Ice sent some names over for domestic help as well, but the biggest thing right away is making decisions on what, where, and how."

That sent them all back into a major discussion on the uses of rooms and the best places to set things up. In the middle of the chaos, when the door opened, Terk stopped, turned, and there was Levi, grinning at him. And right beside him was Stone and Merk and behind them was Rhodes.

"Would you look at that? The four originals."

"It would be five, if Ice had her way," Levi said, "but she's needed at home with Hunter and the baby."

"Of course she is." Terk walked over and greeted the rest. He shared a hug with his brother. There would always be room here for his brother, no matter what.

"Wade, add guest rooms to the list," Terk called out, then greeted Stone and Rhodes with a hearty man hug and slaps on the back.

Meanwhile Levi stood in the middle of the cavernous

room, a look of disbelief on his face. "This really is a castle, isn't it?" Levi asked.

"It really is," Terk replied, with a chuckle, "and we'll have an enormous headache trying to get it outfitted properly."

"Maybe so," his brother murmured, as he walked around, "but, even if it is, this is a huge boon."

"That's how I've been trying to think of it but honestly? At this point in time I'm not so sure." He raised his palms. "We're just getting started on figuring out what room should be assigned where, going by the blueprints."

"I want to see this place. Can we get a tour?" Merk asked. "Maybe at the same time, you can sort out what rooms you're trying to get figured out."

And, with that, the whole group of them went through the main floor and then downstairs. When they walked into the room that Gage and Wade had suggested as an armory, Levi walked around it twice.

"Yeah, definitely an armory." He nodded. "If you look at the weaponry still on the walls, clearly in its glory days, that's what this room was before." Most of the arms were old and not even useable anymore, but, even so, they were still remnants of the finer art of weaponry. "This is fascinating," Levi murmured, as he wandered around. "I mean, I don't envy you the work of getting it set up but sure love the whole look of the place."

"It's definitely special," Terk murmured, "and we have Charles to thank for the idea." He looked over at his friend.

"Hey," Charles replied, with a stately nod, "this has been for sale for quite a while and had always struck me as the perfect layout for something like this."

"Beyond perfect," Levi agreed. "It's stunning."

Just then, Tasha and several of the women, including an older one, came to join them. The older woman flashed a bright smile at the group.

Charles stepped forward to her and reached out his hands. "Emmeline, there you are, my dear."

She walked closer and into his arms for a chaste greeting.

EMMELINE FELT A homecoming that she hadn't experienced in a very long time.

Charles looked at her gently. "So glad you could come back. Now these are more of my friends, and they aren't scary."

"In my experience, your friends are often scary," she countered, laughing, "and so were Dean's." She turned to look at everybody, still with a big smile.

"Hello, Emmeline," Terk said. "Welcome back."

"Sorry to just appear uninvited, but Charles asked that I come to see if you could use my help."

"What?" Terk stopped, looked over at Charles, then back at her. "I'm sure Charles had an excellent reason to suggest it, though he hasn't yet filled us in on it."

"Oh dear," Emmeline said, looking over at Charles in dismay.

He chuckled. "She has a lot of expertise in setting up houses. She has been known to establish some of the great ones in our line."

"Oh, please." She gave an eye roll. "I haven't done that kind of work in a very long time, at least not professionally. I have done projects for several friends more recently."

"Is that really a thing?" Terkel looked over at her in surprise.

"No, not necessarily," she said, with a shake of her head. "I just mean that, when we take on these old buildings, certain things have to be done," she explained. "If the work is done correctly from the start, they can be beautiful and highly functional treasures. If not, they end up as dreary, damp, depressing old relics."

At that, Levi's face cleared from the confusion. "I see exactly what you mean. Terk, you're out of your element here. You've got to trust Charles and Emmeline." Levi looked over at Charles with admiration. "How is it that you never seem to be short of people and always manage to come up with exactly what we need?"

"Hey, it's my business. Remember?" Charles chuckled.

"I know. It's just amazing how it always seems to be just the right match." Levi looked over at Terkel and smacked him on the shoulder. "Hey, Charles has got this. Let's carry on with the tour and see what else we can sort out in the rest of these rooms." And, with that, Terk shrugged, and the group moved off.

CHARLES LEFT THEM to it; then he turned to look at Emmeline. "Thank you for coming."

She smiled. "I'm here, though I'm not sure that this is exactly where I'm needed. Is there a reason you didn't mention it when we were here earlier, when I met Terk and Celia before?"

"That was far too premature, my dear, but I did want you to get a look. Come now. Let's follow along on the tour, and you'll get a better idea of the scope of the project."

As they continued, she gasped at how huge the place really was. "This is even more beautiful than I remember," she exclaimed with delight.

"It is one of the nicest estates," Charles agreed.

"I don't even think that's the right word for it," she said, with a note of envy. "It's brilliant really. So how will they set it up?" As she listened to what Charles shared, she was quite surprised. "Well, I wasn't expecting that. It's very James Bond*ish* of Terk."

"Exactly."

She turned to face Charles and smiled. "And, of course, they all know what you do, … right?"

"Of course they do. However, they don't know anything about what Dean did."

"That's probably for the best. Dean's time has been and gone," she said comfortably.

"And are you handling it better now?"

"I probably wasn't handling it at all back then, but, yes, I am doing much better now." She smiled at him. "Thank you so much for all the support. Mourning and learning to live alone are quite challenging."

"Dean was my best friend, as well as yours," he reminded her, feeling awkward and slightly uncomfortable.

Her face fell ever-so-slightly. "I know he was," she murmured, "and you must miss him terribly too. I've been so thankful for our friendship, since we shared the knowledge of what a wonderful man Dean was."

"Absolutely." Charles wasn't exactly sure what had happened to his normal aplomb when it came to this woman, but, ever since his best friend had passed on, Charles hated this sense of it now being his turn. The two men had been great friends, and the three of them had done so much together, when they could. Now it almost felt like he was stepping on toes that he had no business stepping on.

She looked over at him. "Will you be staying here?"

"Occasionally perhaps, but I still have my set of town-homes in the city."

"Of course. So, if I were to work here, would I be staying here?"

He nodded. "At least until you get it set up, and then you could decide what you want to do after that."

"It'll take quite a bit of staff to run this place," she murmured. "Once it's sorted out, up and running, it will be fine, but to get it to that point could be pretty rough."

"I agree with you there. They will handle all the weaponry and security, but it's the matter of handling the house that will get interesting. There are quite a few women involved now too."

Emmeline winced at that. "Sometimes that doesn't always go over too well."

"And I'm not sure whether or not they have any one person designated for handling this, but I know we definitely have one who is a chef, but, of course, she'll need some help."

"Of course. I think you'll need to have multiple staff here on a permanent basis."

"And they may need to come back and forth, just from the security point of view."

"I do have a few suggestions that I might share, but, first off, this place needs a major cleaning." She stopped and frowned, as she looked up at the curtains still hanging here. "How much upgrade needs to be done on the electrical systems?"

"I don't think the electrical is bad, but definitely things

need to be upgraded."

"Right." She extended a hand and asked, "Have you got a piece of paper, so I can start a list?"

Laughing, he brought out a little notebook from his pocket. "How about this?"

"Perfect." She accepted it with a grin and started writing things down. Then she stopped, looked at him, and asked, "Will the budget be a challenge?"

"I don't think so, at least not for the initial setup. After that, there could be some concerns, until they can get themselves running."

She nodded. "Sounds like fun," she murmured. "And brings back a lot of memories."

"Of course it does. This is similar to what Dean did all around the world."

"Yes, setting up embassies, British Embassies." She nodded. "And then he handled the safe houses for a while there too."

"Yes, but it's the same kind of thing here," Charles murmured. "And once you set up something like that, it still requires somebody to provide oversight and to ensure it's all functioning properly."

"These appear to be very capable people," she whispered, as they wandered ever-so-slightly behind the larger group. She walked with a limp, though it didn't seem to slow her down too much. The group, clearly enjoying the tour and still happily exclaiming over everything, got really excited in one room. "What's all that about?" Emmeline asked.

"Sounds like they are thinking of this as a good spot for the jail, like secure holding cells," Charles explained.

She stepped closer and looked around at the room in question and nodded. "Not exactly what I was thinking they would need though," she noted cautiously.

"They will. No doubt about it."

"Okay," she murmured and kept on walking behind the group.

By the time they finally finished the tour of the upper and lower floors, Charles could almost feel a sense of normality returning to his relationship with Emmeline, which was strange. Seeing her again had sent him off-kilter a little bit, just as it had the last time. They had now returned to investigate the main floor, and he led her into the huge main kitchen.

Emmeline stood in the middle of the room, a big smile on her face.

"This room seems to have made you happy," Charles remarked to Emmeline.

"I do love to cook. And this is the epitome of a perfect place to cook."

At that, a woman from the other side of the kitchen spoke up. "I don't know how much cooking you like to do," she said, "but I'm just tired enough that I could use some help."

Charles joined Mariana with her son and introduced Emmeline to them. Charles explained, "I was hoping that maybe you guys would consider taking her on as a consultant to help you get this place organized."

Mariana looked at him in delight. "Oh, say yes, please say yes," she murmured.

"Are you talking about me or Terkel?" Emmeline asked, with a laugh.

"I don't know. Either, both, whatever," Mariana murmured. "This is just such a huge undertaking. I've only ever operated in a really well-established kitchen, so this is already challenging me."

"But you're definitely up for the challenge, my dear," she said. "Clearly you've already been doing a lovely job, or you wouldn't be in this position."

"Feels like I haven't done anything yet," Marianna murmured. "And believe me. A lot needs to be done here."

"There is. Absolutely there is," Emmeline agreed, "but it's not all bad. There's just a lot of it."

At that, Terk walked over to join them. "Do you see places you think you can help us with?"

"Absolutely." Then she hesitated. "The thing is ..." And then she turned to Charles, who shrugged.

"What's the problem?" Terk asked.

"It's not a problem, but a place like this needs a lot of work and, early on, a lot of organization. I would need to have a bit of a free hand."

Terk frowned and stared at her for a moment. "And, if you had that free hand, what would you do?"

"I'd start by hiring staff to thoroughly clean the place, top to bottom. We'd also have to get the electrical checked, along with the plumbing, the gas, and the furnaces. All the systems must be inspected. The chimneys all need to be cleaned and checked, plus we'd need to bring in a contractor to make sure all the roofing is sound and the windows are secure. We don't want to have a draft or any leaks," she added. "This main kitchen needs a massive upgrade, and everything needs to be fully stocked. I would want to double-check the plumbing in the bathroom on the third floor."

He frowned at her. "I don't even remember seeing a bathroom on the third floor." He shook his head. "This house is massive."

"It is massive, and you'll need somebody who can step

up and see what needs to be done and then does it. However, I don't intend on doing any of it myself, in case you thought that was part of the deal. However, I do have an army of people at my disposal."

"Oh, thank heavens for that," Gage said, staring at her in fascination. "So when can you start?"

Emmeline looked at him in surprise, then over at Terkel. "I'm not sure who the boss is or who's handling the money, but I'll need a very large budget."

"How many figures?" Terk asked warily.

"Six. Possibly more, depending on what we find." His eyes widened. She nodded. "That's the problem with taking on a place like this," she warned. "There's a lot of work initially, and then it would ease off. However, in the meantime, there could be ugly repairs to be made that we don't know about yet."

"Okay, but if we start initially with that kind of a figure, I do want a regular accounting, with receipts, so I can see where the money is going." There was almost a hint of desperation in his voice.

Tasha chuckled, as she came up behind him. "I really like this idea, and, yes, obviously we must have a regular accounting. We'll also have to sort out duties and determine who'll handle various aspects of things," she added. "But if Emmeline can get some basic infrastructure things done quickly and help us to get organized and up and running, I'm all for it."

At that, Terk nodded. "And it would take an awful lot of that off our hands, so that we can focus on the things that we need to do." He looked over at her warily. "Some of the rooms will be off-limits."

"Once they're cleaned and inspected, they can be off-limits but not until then. Otherwise you're just fostering rats, mice, and all kinds of other pests in an old place like this, not to mention electrical, gas, and plumbing problems. The dampness has to be dealt with, and that is the problem on the fourth floor, up in the north corner," she added. "I could smell it there." The others all just looked at her.

"I don't expect any of you to understand, but I suspect Charles does." Emmeline turned toward him.

He nodded. "Yes, you've definitely got a leak in the roof up there." He looked over at Terk. "Now, it's not my place to give you any recommendation, but there is a reason why I brought her in."

"Of course." Terk looked over as another person entered the room. With a wave of relief, he said, "I'm not at all sure Celia will wants to have anything to do with this, but, if she could even be a go-between, that would be awesome. And, with that, he tried to back away.

Celia walked forward, a determined look in her eyes. She then frowned at Terk. "As long as I get a lab out of this deal, I'll be happy to take care of the household account and act as a middleman—a liaison, if you will—with Emmeline, but please do not conclude in any way, shape, or form that I won't be spending the bulk of my time doing my own work."

He grinned at her. "You'll be spending the bulk of your time looking after babies," he clarified, with a chuckle.

"And you?" she asked, raising an eyebrow.

"Will be helping. With two of them, we won't have much choice."

At that, Emmeline turned around in delight. "Are you carrying twins?"

Celia beamed. "I am. We need a nursery soon too. And,

as you can see, outside of Mariana, we're largely ill-equipped to handle this large of an undertaking. We all have a variety of skills, but, as far as starting from scratch with a huge old house like this, we have very little to no experience."

Tasha laughed. "There are certain aspects that we can cover and things we specialize in. And they are things of a sensitive nature of course."

"But beyond that," Celia said, "none of us has the expertise to take a lead role on this, and frankly it's just bigger than us."

"Exactly." Emmeline smiled. "So give it some thought, and you can contact me in a few days and let me know what you've decided."

"I've already thought about it," Celia said, as she turned to face Terk. "Say yes, please." He looked at her in surprise, and she just nodded. "He says yes," Celia stated, as she turned back to Emmeline and beamed.

Emmeline took one look, from Terk to Celia, then burst out laughing. "Oh, I do love it," she said warmly. "You guys will have a lot of fun getting set up."

"I'm not so sure about that." Terk studied the space. "Yet it will be fun to sort out our relationships." He looked over at Charles and gave him a quick nod.

Charles suggested, "I can handle the accounting, if you want. She can send everything to me, and I'll send you a summary on a weekly basis."

"That would be even better," Celia cried out, "just in case I sleep my way through the next month or so."

"Oh dear, let's hope you don't do that," Emmeline noted, "because I'm not kidding. There will be a lot of work to be done that will require a small army of people, and, to a certain extent, they'll be noisy."

"Sure, but an awful lot of rooms are here. Surely there will be one that I can sleep in without too much disturbance."

"We can make sure that we have at least … ah, what?" She looked around, mentally counting the people before her. "Eight rooms for sleeping?"

Terkel stopped, thought about it for a few moments, then shook his head. "Twenty-two bedrooms is what's coming to mind for me." At that, everybody turned and looked at him. He shrugged. "That's the number." He didn't care to explain. He looked over at Celia, who nodded.

Celia added, "As we configure the rooms, especially for those of us who are living here, we should choose the larger options, with en suite bathrooms, of course, and end up with something more like suites. That's a lot of working bathrooms needed at the start," she noted, "and a lot of plumbing to be installed or repaired and then looked after. So we need to note which are primary suites, which are the priority for those of us who are already here, and then the secondary guest suites, and finally the future housing," she explained, understanding fully where Terkel was going apparently.

"It will be chaos for the first few months," Levi noted, now laughing, "and then, before you know it, it'll be more or less done, and you guys will have an incredible place."

Tasha huffed. Loudly. "You want to know chaotic? Try setting up in a bare storage unit complex, with absolutely nothing to start with, while under constant attack, with an ever-growing group of people who were, shall we say, not in the best of shape." Tasha looked from one male team member to the other.

The room was silent for a moment, then Terk nodded.

"That's a pretty generous description, as I recall."

"Agreed. Jesus, what a shitshow," Sophia added. Someone starting laughing, and soon they all were cracking up, and the pressure of the task before them was suddenly relieved—temporarily.

"Thank you, Tasha, for that unfortunate trip down memory lane," Terk said to another chorus of chuckles. "While the task before us is monumental and will undoubtedly be mind-boggling at times, we have a plan for a path forward, and we'll do what we always do. Put the right people in the right positions and work together. We'll get through it."

"It will be a monumental task," Emmeline agreed, "but not to worry. That's why you have me. I'm really quite excited about this." She clapped her hands, beaming. "So, we are agreed?"

They nodded.

"In that case, whatever security process you plan to require for everybody who'll be coming through the castle, it needs to be put in place tonight because I'll have a team in here tomorrow." And, with that, she grabbed Charles by the arm. "Charles, I think you and I need to talk."

Then the two of them disappeared.

CHARLES WALKED INTO the empty servants' kitchen, made a pot of tea, and then sat down with her at the ramshackle table. "What is it you wanted to discuss, my dear?"

"I'll need help," she said immediately.

He nodded. "Of course. I do have some commitments right now though." He was a little cautious about overcommitting.

"I'm not sure there'll be much in the way of running water or anything else here for the next few days," she shared.

"Ah." Charles laughed. "You are more than welcome to stay with me of course."

"Perfect," she said cheerfully. "That's what I wanted to know."

"I'm not sure how they'll feel about not having you on site though."

"And they'll deal with it, when they figure it out," she said, without missing a beat. "I would love to have more to do with this place as time goes on, but it needs to be in an overseer-type position."

"I understand," Charles replied.

She looked at him, smiled. "Now, how have you been faring?"

He looked at her, his eyebrows raised. "Do I look that frail?"

"No, not at all, but then Dean was a little older than you."

"He was, and you are quite a bit younger than both of us," he admitted.

"I've always loved older men," she said, with a grin.

"And I know that you were a huge blessing to Dean," he murmured, unsure where this conversation was going.

"One thing I do need to have is a room for the night and transportation. I was dropped off by a cab."

"Ah, we can handle both of those. Are you sure you don't want to stay here?"

"I will at some point," she murmured, "but I really do want to sort out that bathroom situation first."

He burst out laughing. "You're not the only one, I'm sure. A lot of women are here, and they'll all want the plumbing dealt with quickly."

"Yes, and we'll get there. I've got a plumber, two electricians, and someone to check out the walls, plus pest control, all coming tomorrow—or I will, as soon as I give them the word."

"Give them the word then." He smiled. "I know everybody here is more than anxious to get started."

CHAPTER 2

E MMELINE WAS TOTALLY excited about getting involved in this project and yet found it odd. She had no business being this enthusiastic, but it was hard not to be, after seeing all these younger people with so much to give in their lives and all the new beginnings they had. She'd heard a bit about them from Charles, and, of course, he had a very different view of them, as a lot of people would. But she trusted Charles all the same, just as she'd always trusted her partner, Dean.

Dean had been older, enough older that her parents had been against the two of them marrying. She hadn't listened and had never regretted it. Sometimes one had to do what one had to do. In her case follow her heart. Generations did not have to be a barrier to love, and it's not as if that many years were between them anyway. He was fourteen years older, and they had enjoyed over twenty years together.

WITH THE WORK here at the castle already underway, the days took on a life of their own, as Emmeline brought in team after team after team. But then she knew the teams to contact. She knew the specialists, and they all had their own teams as well. By the time the first week of mostly cleaning and inspections were over, she had a full assessment of the work that needed to be done. She sat here at the table in the main kitchen, looking at her list and the estimates.

When Celia walked in a little bit later and noted Emmeline seated here, Celia admitted, "A part of me says I should run, but, at the same time, I feel like I should sit down and see how you're doing."

Emmeline looked up and grinned. "And believe me. I understand both sentiments." She chuckled. "How are the babies doing?"

"Babies are fine." Celia smiled, patting her tummy. "I'm still getting used to the idea of two."

"Good luck with that."

"I'll admit that it took me awhile. Do you have children?"

"No, my first husband couldn't have any, though honestly I think he was happy with that." She looked over at Celia, smiled. "My husband was quite a bit older, which caused my family some trouble, but I was okay with it."

"I don't think love requires a common age between the parties, does it?" Celia asked.

"No, it absolutely doesn't, and I was quite devastated when I lost him last year. For that, I owe Charles a *thank you* for bringing me in on this project," she shared. "Honestly it's been a great way to feel alive and useful again."

"I'm so happy to hear that. As I already told Charles, neither Terkel nor I have any living parents, so we were hoping that he would stick close to our babies, so they would have something akin to a grandparent."

Emmeline smiled at her. "What a lovely thought for all concerned. Now, not to change the subject, but we need to see to a ton of work, which needs to be done here first, hopefully before the twins arrive."

Celia pulled up a chair and sat down beside her. "So, what have you got?" she murmured. By the time they went through all the facts and figures, her mind reeled. "Do you have people capable of doing all these repairs?"

"Yes, and for the next couple weeks, it will be pretty intense, but that is necessary to get it all done as quickly, efficiently, and expertly as possible. Three of the bathrooms need complete renovations. Those are big jobs, and they won't fit within this budget," Emmeline explained. "Most of the other bathrooms will need work as well but are definitely within the scope of this initial effort."

"So it comes down to setting priorities then," Celia recapped, "which is pretty easy. The roof, the electrical, and the plumbing."

At that point, Mariana walked in. "Make sure the main kitchen is part of that."

"Don't worry. This kitchen has already been approved, and the work should be underway soon." Emmeline smiled at her. "We'll be hitting it hard over the next few days with demolition, plumbing, and electrical, and that could cause some further trouble, since we never quite know what we'll find. Hopefully not too much that we don't already know about."

"*Hopefully,*" Mariana repeated. "And we're getting by with the small servants' kitchen for now, and that is already fully stocked. So we're doing okay, and, with any luck, things will go quickly in here."

"We've got a big team coming in soon just for this kitchen," Emmeline announced, "so I think I can get it done quickly." And she was so up for the challenge.

BY MIDDAY, SHE sat down at the dining table with the rest of the group, feeling much better about everything, as she already had multiple things checked off on her list. Meaning, many tasks were delegated to her teams now.

A few minutes later, she looked up to see that Charles had just arrived. She smiled at him, as he walked over, took a seat beside her, and waved his hand, saying, "Don't stop on my account. Keep eating, everyone."

"I wasn't expecting to see you today." Emmeline smiled his way.

"I wasn't expecting to be here"—he laughed—"but honestly, curiosity got the better of me."

She burst out laughing.

"And how addictive that is," he said, with a grin.

She smiled. "It's more than addictive. Just being here is addictive."

Charles looked around and asked, "How are things going for everyone?"

With that, Terk launched into a summary, which Gage picked up and added to.

Then Mariana joined in. "I'll be glad when the main kitchen is ready," she noted, "although the small servants' kitchen is kind of nice for just us. But honestly, I can't wait to get the big one up and going."

"And maybe with that," Terk suggested, "you should be hiring cooking staff first."

"Maybe." Mariana looked over at Celia.

"I'm trying to convince Emmeline to stay on for a bit," Celia explained immediately. "She's the one who cooked dinner tonight."

Charles looked at her in surprise. "How on earth did you find the time to do that?"

She laughed. "I felt like cooking, but I don't want to do it full-time."

"No, of course not, but it is nice that you got to give it a go tonight."

"It is, indeed," she replied, yet suddenly aware that something was off in his voice. And his excuse for showing up didn't necessarily wash.

Terkel looked at Charles for a long moment, his gaze intense. "All right, Charles. You should probably tell us, whatever it is."

Charles frowned. "Are you sure?"

"Yes, it's better if we all handle this kind of stuff together."

At that, everybody froze, putting down their forks and turning their attention to Charles. They might not all know him well enough to note when something was off, but they certainly knew Terk.

"I presume this isn't something we'll want to hear," Calum said.

"It's definitely something I wish I didn't have to tell you, but you do need to know. I've just come from MI6, and one of the men they took away from your lovely nightmare has escaped custody during a facility transfer."

"What?" Tasha exclaimed. "There's only one left alive. Bill, Camo Guy? How is that even possible?"

"That remains to be determined, but unfortunately, my dear, it has happened. Believe me when I say that they're not very happy about it. He was being transported at the time. This particular prisoner was thought to be of zero account. Instead he appears to have had more in the way of connections than we realized."

"Crap," someone said, as the others expressed similar sentiments.

"Any reason to suggest we're in danger?" Mariana asked, brushing an errant lock of hair from Little Cal's face.

"A specific reason? No, but is there any reason *not* to consider yourselves in danger?"

Predictably they all looked over at Terk.

He smiled. "You all have just as many senses as I do. Maybe we should do a callout right now. Who's picking up on what?"

"I'm picking up nothing," Cara murmured.

"Me neither," Clary admitted immediately, "but I'm exhausted, using my energy helping *some* people who shouldn't be doing nearly as much as they are." She grinned at several of the male team members.

They all just grinned back at her. "Yeah, but, because of you, at least we're getting somewhere," one of them said with a smile, as others chimed in their agreement.

"Yeah, and you're wearing me out," she muttered.

This was something that Emmeline was still struggling to adjust to. This entire group shared unusual and unique abilities, which made them all very special and helped her to understand why security was even more important here. Charles had alluded to it but not in specific terms. The fact that somebody was loose again was definitely disconcerting. "I can't bring workers onto this property if they're not safe," she stated.

"No, of course not," Charles agreed. "I don't believe that is an issue at this point, but we can't be sure, which frankly is an inherent risk of the business. What we do need to do is be aware that this man is out there."

"Yes." Terk nodded. "We'll take care of it."

Emmeline detected something off or different in his voice. She didn't understand what it meant, but, when Charles nodded at her in a reassuring manner, she realized that nobody here would be too bothered by it all. "I gather I don't know about things here, but, as long as you tell me that it's safe, then I'll trust you."

"It's safe," Terkel confirmed immediately.

She laughed. "Is it, or do you just want to have your house in order?"

"That too," he agreed, with a nod. "But we, *you* have already accomplished an amazing amount of work in the time that you've been here."

"Not me, the workers, but the freedom you've given me has helped, and we've gotten a lot cleared off our list already. Give me another month, and we'll have everything up and running, including staff hired, if you'll tell me what your budgets are for that too."

"I have no idea," Terk replied in consternation, "but let's reverse engineer that. How much staff do you think we need?"

"Well," she began, "if you don't want them living on the complex, then you could probably have an army of cleaners come in once every week, which would minimize traffic in and out, which might be helpful from a security standpoint. Other than that, I think you probably need two to three people in the kitchen. But it's hard to say at this point."

"Why do you say that?"

"If it's just eight or ten of you here," she explained, "that's not all that bad to cook for three meals every day." She looked over at Mariana. "However, I don't think Mariana is too interested in taking that job on permanently."

41

"For a little while, I can do it for sure," she said cheerfully, "particularly if you'll give me that kick-ass kitchen I've been seeing sneak peeks of." The two women exchanged knowing glances.

"Right, there's nothing like new toys," Emmeline stated.

Mariana nodded. "I could manage the kitchen, and surely do some cooking, but we'll definitely need to bring in other people to maintain the ability to right-size, depending on how many we're feeding. One cook for sure, possibly an assistant, and maybe combine those two with other prep staff and kitchen cleaning crews as well, if needed."

That brought the discussion to a whole new level.

TERK FELT HIMSELF sinking under the details. When he looked over at Celia, she chuckled.

"It'll be fine."

"Says you," he murmured. Everybody had some idea about the money, and it was a vast number sitting in the account, but he also knew that to set up and to outfit this company the way they needed to, they would run through money at an alarming rate that nobody would really see coming. He had to make sure it was enough to get set up and to see this through as they sought paying security jobs. As he pondered all that, he felt a small hand joining his. Celia had moved closer to put her hand in his. "Terkel is worried about money," she spoke up to everyone. "But I can tell you that it's fine. There is more than enough to outfit this property."

"Do you think so?" Terk asked, looking at her.

She nodded. "Absolutely, but you might have to consider that, with this new scenario, we'll have to raise the budget or the timeline on the security."

"We're already on that," he murmured. He looked over at the others to confirm, and they nodded. "Some things are just not negotiable when it comes to this timeline."

She nodded. "See? You'll be fine then, but I can tell that we'll clearly need kitchen help."

And that's where the conversation returned to later on, well after lunch, when most of the women had chosen to get up and leave the men to their security conversation.

Charles spoke up. "Are you okay with the budget?"

"It's being decimated at a rate I hadn't really expected," Terk replied, "but it's not my field. So it is what it is. I can't imagine how this would look today if we hadn't had Emmeline leading the charge."

"No doubt." Levi nodded. "Terk, one of the biggest things is learning the business aspects of the thing, right? But, for now, you're in good hands, and you just have to go with the flow to get everything set up. After that, you can work out a budget and tweak things, like staffing levels as you need to. This isn't the time or the place right now. Particularly"—he turned to look at Charles—"when Charles is holding something back."

"Now what is that which you didn't want to bring up with everyone here?" Terk asked.

Charles winced. "I didn't want to say anything, until I had a chance to talk to you about it. I've had an update, and apparently the latest word from MI6 is that they're looking for the escaped prisoner, of course, but their best intel had them believing that he's headed this way."

"And, if he's heading this way, that means he knows we're here." Terk nodded calmly. His mind was already full of what they would need to do to get this op set up. "Any ETA?"

"I'm not sure," Charles replied, "but you and I both know that it wouldn't matter. Once somebody's got it in their head that they'll come here, then they'll get here on their time frame."

"And do we have any idea on the agenda of what they're after?"

"I don't think so, except that some of the contracts on your team may not have been canceled just because the original people who put them out there are no longer with us."

"Right, somebody must have confirmed this contract on us is still live, right?"

Charles murmured, "Exactly, and, in this case, I think we're safe to say that whoever put the contract out on your team won't be paying anymore."

"But that doesn't mean we don't still have people after us though, right?" Gage groaned. "That's just depressing."

And, with that, silence fell on the group.

CHAPTER 3

EMMELINE HEARD CHARLES speaking to the team afterward, even though he had done his best to keep his voice low. As soon as the conversation was over, the men gathered around and tried to come up with a defensive strategy. She completely ignored them, knowing that they would do whatever they could do to fix this and that there wasn't much that anybody else could do. But one of the lessons she had learned over the years of her marriage to Dean was that some things just couldn't be avoided, and things would happen, regardless of what she did. So she might as well just keep doing what she was doing and hope that this resolved itself. Just because some guy escaped custody didn't mean he was coming here. But it also didn't mean he wasn't.

By the time the day began to wind down, she sat in the working servants' kitchen at a table that one of her teams had hastily put together from an auction house. It was huge, twenty-plus feet huge. And it would go into the large great room when it was finished. She had several notepads in front of her that she was trying to collate into an organized list. Mariana was preparing the next meal. Emmeline looked over at her and frowned. "If you need a hand with dinner, just let me know."

"I'm okay for the moment," she said cheerfully. "Besides,

I've got Little Calum's help."

Emmeline looked over to see the little boy, sitting up on the end of the counter, munching away on something. "With help like that, I'm sure you'll be fine."

Mariana laughed. "I don't know about that, but, for the moment, with it just being a few of us who are here now, I'm fine."

"Of course you are," she murmured, "but I can always make a dessert if you need something."

"It's not that we *need* something," she said, looking at her with interest, "but honestly desserts have a lot to do with keeping spirits up."

"Isn't that an amazing thing too." Emmeline walked closer to the counter. "What do we have for supplies though?"

"Not a whole lot," Mariana admitted. "I did have them bring in a bunch of basics, so we could put things together as needed. It just depends on what you have in mind."

"How about just a quick coffee cake?" she suggested. "Nothing too fancy, just some crumble for the topping maybe, heavy in whatever spices we have." She looked over at Mariana expectantly.

"You go for it, and, if you are making something like that, I don't know whether or not it's a bigger deal for you, but I always tend to do a double or triple batch, so we have more for later."

"Oh, I can get behind that idea too." Emmeline reached for the mixer they had picked up from the commercial kitchen store, along with a lot of the other ingredients. "Will you need the mixer in the next little while?"

"Nope, go ahead," Mariana replied. "The mashed potatoes are already done. They're in the oven with cheese."

"Sounds lovely." Emmeline reached for the flour. She'd been baking for a long time and had several good favorites that had held her in good stead over the years. It also meant she didn't need a recipe, and that was a plus right now.

As she worked, Mariana asked, "How are you doing on your work list?"

"It's going," she quipped, with a laugh. "We've got six more people coming in tomorrow. We're getting through the cleaning upstairs, and working our way through to the middle floors. I've got plumbers and electricians and a couple carpenters working on the upper floor, also working their way down."

"Interesting you started on the upper floor," Mariana noted.

"It seemed prudent to fix the roof leak and the outside walls and then work our way downward. Plus, I was trying to get things accomplished without too many interruptions, and, with Terk's team everywhere, the interruptions were getting to be a problem."

"Right, everybody's here, but they don't necessarily have their own spaces yet, so I notice people don't really quite know where to stay. I'm kind of hiding out in this servants' kitchen because it gives me a place to just exist without having to move around every five minutes to get out of somebody's way. Seems like an odd problem to have in a place this massive."

Emmeline nodded her agreement. By the time she had the batter mixed up, she asked, "Gosh, I didn't even think of this beforehand, but do we have baking dishes?"

"Yes." Mariana laughed and pointed. "Right here in our enormous pantry." She chuckled when the doors were opened to reveal mostly empty shelves. "This won't be empty for very long." She brought out several loaf pans and a few cake pans and some large muffin tins. "How many do you need?"

"Probably all of those," Emmeline said. "I ended up making a quadruple batch. I wasn't sure the mixer would handle it, but it looks like you've got something with some legs."

Mariana smiled. "Knowing that Terk's plan involves having more people here, I wanted to be sure we had equipment that would hold up to that over time. And frankly the secret to producing larger quantities with a small staff is being organized, doing prep work in advance, and having larger commercial-size equipment."

As she listened, Emmeline managed to dump the batter into four different pans, with even enough for a small one afterward. She pointed to the little cake and looked at Little Calum. "That's his for later, okay?"

The little boy beamed, as Mariana smiled and shot Emmeline a grateful look. "He'll love that," she murmured. "Thank you."

"I thought he might," Emmeline replied. As if knowing that they were talking about him, Little Calum came racing over, saw the baby cake pan, and stopped to cry with delight.

"It's got to cook first though," Emmeline said calmly, as she started loading up the oven. And, with that done and the timer set, she went back to the table and her list. The whole time she'd been baking, her mind had been inundated with things that still needed to be done. As soon as she got everything written down and sorted, she looked around at what else she could do.

"Are you looking for more things to do already?" Mariana asked.

Emmeline nodded. "I find, when I do something different, it helps me to just detach a bit, and all these other things I've forgotten pop to the surface. So then I write them down, and they don't get forgotten."

"If you're looking for something else to dull your brain into submission," she suggested, "I've got vegetables to be prepped."

"Absolutely. What are we doing with them?"

"I've got two roasts in right now, and we've got the mashed potatoes in. So would you chop a big salad? Meanwhile I'm cooking extra potatoes for a potato salad for tomorrow." She pointed to a massive pot on the back burner. "We'll just do it rustic style, so I didn't peel them. I've got hard-boiled eggs happening for that as well. However, we need more veggies for dinner."

"Perfect, so how about I just whip up a pot of steamed vegetables?"

"That sounds great, thank you."

"How long until you want to serve?"

"About thirty minutes." Mariana glanced over at her. "The roasts are almost done, but I'll take them out in a few minutes to let them rest."

And, with that, Emmeline got busy on the vegetables. Without all the noise of the mixer and their own conversation, she heard the men still talking in a nearby room.

"I don't know what's going on with them," Mariana stated out loud.

"MI6 believes Bill, the guy who escaped, could be headed this way," Emmeline said calmly.

At that, Mariana looked at her and gasped. "Seriously?"

"Yeah."

"And it doesn't bother you that somebody could be

coming here after us?"

"It's the same work my husband was in all the time, so I am quite used to the danger factor."

"How did you learn to handle it?" Mariana asked.

"You'd be surprised at how much that kind of danger surrounds us all the time. We just aren't aware of it. Things will calm down here, once you get settled in. Right now though, because you're coming fresh from all those other problems, you haven't had that dose of normality yet. It's coming, and that will really help."

"Will it?" Mariana asked in wonder. "Sometimes I don't even know what I got myself into."

"I wouldn't worry about it, dear. By the time you have it figured out, the guys will have it all sorted. I think, if we each just do our jobs and do what we can to pitch in, it will all work out for everyone."

"I hope so," Mariana murmured. "You're awfully calm."

"I've got quite a few more years of experience." She chuckled.

"You wear it beautifully." Mariana hesitated, then asked, "Are you and Charles close?"

"Oh, yes, Charles is an old friend. He and my husband were best friends as well."

"That's interesting."

"We've all been best friends since forever," she said, with a wave of her hand.

"But that doesn't necessarily tell me what your relationship is now." Mariana giggled.

Emmeline flushed. "Very subtle. *Not.* Anyway, I don't think Charles is ready for anything more than friendship, and, after only one year as a widow, I'm not sure I am either."

"I can tell you that Charles definitely is ready, but he's respecting your space." Mariana gave her a gentle smile.

"If that's the case, I guess we'll get to it when this is more or less calmed down. I'll be here for at least one more month, until everything is sorted."

"The fact that you even took it on is huge," Marianna noted. "We would have muddled through and figured it out but not nearly so efficiently and definitely not this quickly."

"It's something that's within my wheelhouse, which makes all the difference. I'll be happy to help out once you guys get up and running, and, by then, you might have a better idea of what your needs are."

"Maybe. We'll need kitchen help for sure though. Otherwise I'll be cooking all the time."

"Did you work before?"

"I did and still have some online companies," Mariana replied, "and, yes, cooking part-time could be a job, but we'll have to figure it out. It also depends on how they decide to run the company. If it'll be more of a co-op situation—where everybody shares in the funds at the end of the day and all the expenses come off the top—then everybody all pitches in equally and gets a portion. The other option is that they split it up into paychecks, and it would be Terk's company."

"Now that's interesting. I've never even thought of something like that. It all depends on what works for you guys. It comes down to whatever you want to make happen." And, with that, she turned and presented the large bowl of veggies. "If you think the timing is right, I'll put these on."

"Yeah, go ahead."

And, with that, Emmeline took the vegetables over to the stove. As they steamed, she began carrying the other food to the table, which soon filled up quickly. Veggies done, she put them in a large bowl and took them to the table, ready to sit down, only to find Charles seated already. She looked over at him and smiled. "Nice to see you again. Did you even get a chance to leave here today?"

He shook his head. "Nope, not yet." He patted the seat beside him. "I see you jumped back into the kitchen again."

"I do like to cook." She gave him a gentle smile, as she sat beside him. "You know that."

"Of course I do. I also know that these guys are grateful and very lucky to have you helping out."

"I don't know. I'll also charge them a lot for my work." Then she burst into a beautiful bright laughter.

Terkel looked over, grinning. "And I expect that too. Nobody here works for free."

"That will be an interesting thing for you all to sort out," she noted, as she thought about Mariana's question. "Everybody was getting paychecks and had their own money and did whatever they were doing in their lives before this?"

Terk nodded. "And that's something we definitely should have a family discussion about."

"Good. Keep me out of it, please. I'll simply present an invoice, you pay, and we're good."

He chuckled. "Just don't break the bank with it."

"No, not going to, but sometimes you have to charge what you're worth, and that'll be something you guys probably should get some help working out in terms of cost analyses for jobs."

"We'll have to look at it," Terk admitted. "Working for the government, the cost of these things don't really hit you."

"Ice can help you with some of that too," Levi suggested.

"I'd like to say I could help, but she handles most of that."

Merk nodded. "True story. Even when she doesn't, she does. We say we'll do something for somebody, and the next thing we know, there's some kind of negotiation going on for supplies or something that makes sense to everybody, and they're always happy to pay. However she does it, all I know is that it doesn't leave us broke, so it's got to be a good system."

"It's more than a good system." Terkel frowned. "Yet it's hardly my area of expertise."

"Doesn't matter whether it is or not." Merk grinned. "Although maybe your little scientist working with her grant applications and funding budgets might be the best person to keep track of something like that."

"Oh, ouch." Celia winced and frowned at Merk. "Maybe on an interim basis, I can at least review things until we get our pricing systems down on these jobs, but I'm not exactly sure that taking over that kind of stuff is my forte either."

"You'd be surprised at what you can do," Levi said, with a smile.

Dinner was a wonderful and boisterous affair, and, by the time it was done, Emmeline had to admit that she had missed events such as this. She yawned at the table, looked over at Charles, and said, "You'll have to excuse me now. I'll go up to my room and get some rest."

Glancing at his phone, he said, "Wow, it is far later than I thought." He hopped to his feet. "Come on. Let me help you up to your room. You look tired."

"I'm fine, but still, I didn't realize the toll that a year of heavy emotional reactions takes on your energy levels," she murmured. "I thought for sure I would be over all this."

"And is it still emotions?" he asked.

"I don't know. I jumped in with both feet to handle this castle setup, and I don't think I saw ground for quite a while."

He chuckled. "I don't imagine you did. And that's very much *you*, my dear."

"Very much," she admitted, "but it's all good though. They're a wonderful bunch to work with."

"Good." He walked her up to the third floor, noting that her limp was a bit more pronounced, the way it typically got when she overdid it. "Elevators?"

"Yeah, I've got estimates coming in this week. I think it needs to be two, considering security."

He looked at her and grinned. "Did you talk to Terkel about it?"

"He looked haunted, when I mentioned it the last time." She grinned. "I figured that, as soon as I got the estimates, I could sit down and talk to the men as a group. Security will definitely be their prime concern, so it needs to be something that more than one can pitch in with ideas on."

"Maybe the entire group at that," Charles added, pondering it.

"I thought about that too, but then I don't know at what point too many cooks spoil the broth and end up with too many opinions and not enough progress."

He smiled. "That is very true."

CHARLES STAYED AS long as he could before he gave her a gentle smile and a wave. "Remember to rest a little bit tomorrow," he suggested. "Take it a little easy on yourself. This isn't a marathon, after all."

She laughed. "I'm fine."

He turned and walked down to the servants' kitchen area where the guys appeared to be in a meeting, all gathered around the enormous table. He smiled at them. "Good night." And, with a wave, he headed toward the front door.

"Hang on a minute." Terk hopped up, then walked him to the door. "She looked really tired tonight. Is there some health condition we don't know about?"

"No, not at all. At least none that she's told me about," he corrected. "I think she's still dealing with the loss of her husband. And frankly this is the most she's put herself back out in the world since his passing."

"Yeah, that's all quite a process, I understand," he murmured.

Charles looked at him and smiled. "You have no idea," he said gently. "Just treat her nicely, and she'll work her butt off, like you've never seen."

"She already has," he admitted, "and I'd be more than happy if she wants to stay on full-time."

"She might want to, but, between you and me, I'm kind of hoping to convince her to come to my corner."

Terkel studied him and then nodded. "That makes a lot of sense too. Good luck with that."

"Just don't say it in such a way that makes me think I don't have a chance. That sounded a little sarcastic."

"Not at all. It feels pretty solid to me."

Charles looked at him in surprise. "That would be nice. Nothing in life has ever been anything I could particularly count on."

"Because we're always out there, willing to do whatever we need to do to make things happen in our world."

Charles nodded. Pulling open the door, he stepped outside.

A *smack* sounded instantly, and the wood splintered beside his head on the massive front door.

Swearing, Terk grabbed Charles and pulled him inside the door, slamming it shut. "That answers that question," Terk snapped, as he looked down at his friend. "Are you okay?"

"Yes, but we need to warn the others," Charles said.

Terkel smiled. "Already did."

Charles looked at him and frowned. "You really can talk telepathically, can't you?"

"I can," he murmured, "at least with my team, and they're responsible for contacting their partners."

"Of course," he murmured. He looked at the front door. "Well, that's a fine kettle of fish. I was hoping to go home and have a good shot of whiskey."

Terkel studied the light outside and the shadows, as they played across the lawn. "I have some good whiskey upstairs," he replied, but his focus was elsewhere.

"Oh, do you now?" Charles said in appreciation. "In that case, I guess I'm spending the night."

"We do have a couple spare beds."

Terk had just finished saying that, when several men joined them. Levi pulled up the rear. "How do you want to handle it?"

"We need outside reconnaissance, to see if this is one or two." He looked over at the men. "Gage?"

Gage nodded. "Absolutely. I'll take Damon with me." Just like that, the two men headed out one of the north exits.

Rhodes turned to Levi. "You up for coming with me, and we'll take the south?"

"Absolutely."

Terk focused on Wade and Merk. "I want you both to stand guard on the home front."

Wade stepped up, and Merk nodded immediately. "And what about the rest?"

"I've already sent Calum and Rick to our holding cell area to prep for prisoners and have Scott and Brody studying the tunnels. We have a couple dodgy ones down there that we haven't had a chance yet to work on."

Some of the women appeared at that time.

Merk offered to stand guard at the front of the house and was soon off, running.

"We don't even have a standard protocol in place yet," Terk admitted, "but the safest place in the entire house right now is the small servants' kitchen."

"Good," Mariana replied. "In that case, I'll return to where I was to begin with. Come on, Little Calum." Mariana marched determinedly, with the sleepy little boy now in her arms.

Terk studied everybody and realized just how new and different this was for them. "Once we get protocols and proper security in place, it will be a different story next time," Terk promised.

The women slowly nodded.

"Is there anything we can do?" Clary asked.

"Yeah, ready yourselves in case any injuries are coming."

"I'm ready for that," Cara said, with a shrug.

"Anybody picking up anything outside?" Wade asked.

"Yeah." Sophia nodded. "I'm getting two." Terk looked at her in surprise; she shrugged. "I think it's because I'm around you. It's getting even harder to figure out what's new and what's different though," she murmured.

"Even getting that much is pretty amazing," Wade noted.

Sophia asked Terk, "What are you getting?"

"Definitely two, but we can't count out a scenario where they may have more people farther away."

With that, they all disappeared into their designated areas.

Charles stood at Terk's side and frowned. "Is there anything you want me to do?"

Terkel turned to him and nodded. "Roust Emmeline and get her down to the servants' kitchen to stay there with the other women, please."

"Weapons?"

Terk nodded. "Remember the armory, where the old weapons were hung on the walls?"

Charles nodded slowly.

"Take a look in there, and you'll find a spare or two."

AND, WITH THAT, Charles was gone. Knowing that it was important that everybody be where they could be accounted for, he headed for Emmeline's room. When he knocked on the door, his motion hard and crisp, she called out in response. He pushed open the door to see her sitting on the side of the bed, notepads strewn across the mattress.

He smiled. "You'll need to collect all your notes. We're going back down to the servants' kitchen."

"Why's that?" she asked.

"Because, as I was leaving, I got shot at." Even now blood dripped down his temple. "Don't worry. That's from the wood splintering. So everybody has their assignments. Some are out doing reconnaissance, trying to see how many are out there. Those of us staying inside," he added, "are gathering in the smaller kitchen."

"Good enough." She smiled at him. "I'm glad you're staying."

"I wasn't planning on it. I was trying to leave."

"Ah, but trying to leave and getting out are two different things around here. So many times I've tried to leave, and I just never seem to get anywhere. There's always so much work that pulls me back."

"Were you planning on going anywhere in particular?" he asked curiously.

"Not in particular." She laughed. "But I have supplies to get in town, and I need to order some things. Plus, I have to get into the shops and just browse for ideas too." She shrugged. "So I guess that I've been trying to get out for a while."

"It'll be like that for quite a bit longer, I think."

"It will be, but we'll get there eventually," she murmured.

He proceeded to escort her toward the stairs.

"And," she added, "the elevators really must come into play at some point. I don't consider myself old or unfit by any means, but wow. After you've done them a few times, it doesn't seem practical on a daily basis."

"You'll also be surprised at the fitness routine these guys will set up right here on the stairs." Charles chuckled. "You'll find you're at your absolute peak of health. and these stairs that you'd see as a nuisance are, for them, just another way to exercise."

"Good for them," she said, with feeling. "I, on the other hand, am looking forward to swimming in that pool, which I haven't been able to get to either."

He burst out laughing. "It is nice to know that they have as much available here as they do. Everyone should be quite comfortable, when it's finally done."

"They will be. I'll make sure of it. I just don't think anybody realizes how much work is involved in these old places, particularly since we haven't uncovered all the problems yet."

"What are your concerns?"

"Possibly some foundation support, leveling and things of that sort. I'm not terribly happy with the basement. And I'm not even sure that it really is a basement. I found a wine cellar and a couple tunnels under there, but I haven't located where they go. I meant to tell Terkel, but I haven't had a chance yet."

"Whereabouts are the tunnels?" Charles shot her an electric look. "Because, if they end up outside somewhere, and the men don't know about it—"

"Oh, crap," Emmeline said. "That's something I should have updated Terk on immediately."

"I would hope that they already know about it because they have done a full inspection of the property."

"No, I doubt it." She reached up to rub her temple. "I was checking for any wine in the casks, when I realized a door was behind them."

"And did you open it?"

"I did." She looked at him in horror. "Oh, dear."

"In that case, we'll make sure it's closed."

"Did they find any blueprints for this place?" she asked.

"Blueprints of some sort because I know that they had something they were comparing to their physical survey, but that doesn't mean that these tunnels will be noted on there." He led the way down to the armory, or what was left of it, and it didn't take him long to roust a spare handgun.

"Are you allowed to take that?" she asked, fascinated.

He nodded. "Terk told me that it was here."

"You don't have one to spare, do you?" she asked hopefully.

He winced. "I'm sorry, no. There seems to be just the one. If I'd realized …"

"Right, if I'd realized it was that kind of a job, I would have come prepared as well."

"Are your licenses up to date?"

"Sure. That was part of the marriage with Dean. Remember?"

Charles chuckled. "Indeed, I do. His concern over everyone's safety was admirable."

"Yes, it sure was," she said, with a smile. "We had a lot of good years."

"Any regrets marrying him?"

"No, no, none at all." She shook her head. "He wasn't always the easiest person to love, but he was definitely fair, though quite regimented in his outlook in life. But I also had a chance to travel with him, something I may not have done in any other way, and our life itself was quite decent," she shared. "The topic of children was something of a challenge, but, once we just let it go, it ceased to be a problem."

"And I suppose you consider it too late now."

"Yes, I do consider it too late, and, while it might be possible, or there is always adoption, but the question is, will I be around to look after a child? It sounds irresponsible frankly."

"You could always adopt an older child, or you could become an honorary grandparent." At that, he laughed. "I suspect this place will explode with children soon enough."

She smiled. "Won't that be fun?" She tucked her arm

into his, as she led the way down to the cellar. "Having children was one of those things that I often thought about but never really missed—until now that I'm alone. It's amazing just how lonely life can be."

"You are more than welcome to come live with me, my dear."

Charles noted a hesitation in her steps and in her voice when she replied.

"Interesting option."

She had said it in a fairly neutral tone. He was disappointed because this wasn't at all how he wanted to present the idea, so she wouldn't have had any idea how he was thinking about it anyway. "Think about it," he murmured. "We've always been good friends, and I do understand loneliness."

"You understand loneliness," she asked, "but do you understand love?" And then she cried out, "Oh, it's over here, Charles."

She had completely changed the subject, leaving him wondering just what on earth had happened. As soon as they entered the room, he saw what she meant. "Did you move all these?"

She nodded. "I did have a couple people in here helping me for a little bit. Once the big stuff was moved, I sent them off to do something else, so I could get to the rest. Come over here." As she entered the tunnel, they heard a sound on the other end. She gasped.

Charles stepped out in front of her. "Something is here," he murmured, "or someone."

"Maybe, but we also have rats."

He nodded. "A big empty place like this? I'm sure they moved in within days."

She chuckled. "No doubt multiple generations are in here by now."

He stepped around the corner, peering through the darkness. "What about lights?"

She shook her head, as they kept going deeper and deeper into the tunnel. He heard another sound, but this was more like swearing. She reached out a hand to his shoulder, and he nodded. As they crept closer, Charles wished he had let somebody know where they were; that was definitely an issue. But there hadn't been much time, once he realized there could be an underground entrance here that nobody may know about.

In the distance, Charles heard somebody whispering.

"It's right here, just like I told you. I found it the other day."

"Why would they not have found it yet?" somebody asked in a decidedly surly voice. "This is a stupid errand."

"Look. I told you that they'll know about all the other exits because they're on the blueprints. I had a copy of those too."

"Maybe, maybe not," the other guy muttered. "But this place is a mausoleum, and a million places are here for people to hide. No way we'll get in and out. We're much better off finding a place to get at them when they are away from here."

"They're all sitting ducks here," the first man snapped. "Everybody always feels safe in their own homes. They never realize how unprotected they are because they've let down their guard."

"Do you really think these assholes ever let down their guard?"

"They're not Superman or any other kind of superpowered freaks. They're just men."

"Lots of people have been trying to take them out, which goes to my question. Why would they let their guard down here, especially if they know you've escaped?"

"They don't know jack shit. Believe me. They just think they know."

"Of course they know," the second man argued in disgust. "This is stupid, Bill. We're walking into a trap."

"Then go home, just fucking leave, and I'll take care of business myself, but you're sure as hell not getting paid."

"You only pay me peanuts anyway," the other man replied, his voice becoming distant.

"Shit." And that was the only sound they heard, but, for Charles, it was music to his ears. It was one thing to have multiple intruders, but to have just one? Well, that would make Charles's job a hell of a lot easier. Emmeline was off to the side behind him, and, when he held a finger to his lips, she just nodded.

She'd been here before. Her husband had been part of MI6, and they had endured several attacks on his own property over the years. You could always count on her to do the right thing in a scenario like this. However, Charles could imagine she was missing her own weapon pretty badly just now.

As they waited, the other man stumbled through, talking to himself, and swearing.

"Fine, I'll do the damn job myself." At that, he stepped forward and snuck toward the inner doorway to this tunnel. Charles came up behind him and hit his head really hard with the gun. The man crumpled to his knees but didn't go out. Just as he rose to turn and attack, Emmeline came up with a chunk of wood in her hand and hit him hard on the temple, and down he went.

She looked over at Charles and grinned. "Do you think we can get a reward?"

"More like another case of *mind our own business and stay out of the government's business.*"

"Funny how that always ends up being the answer."

"Right, now do you want to have one of the guys summon Terk?"

"Certainly, but let's get this guy secured first. And I'm a little worried about his friend." When Charles raised his eyebrows, she shrugged. "A lot of people are outside, so he may choose to come back this way and hide long enough to protect himself."

"All the more reason for you to take off and get us some backup." Charles efficiently tied up the intruder with tape from one of the boxes found here. "Have you even been into all these boxes?"

"Antiques," she declared. "Probably enough money in these pieces to finance all the renovations," she added, "but I've only just barely scratched the surface." And he could tell from the passionate note in her voice that she was looking forward to that part of the journey as well.

"Wow, they're lucky to have you."

"You keep saying that." She chuckled. "Who are you trying to convince? Them or me?"

"Them. You and I both know your worth," he said calmly.

With a smile, she dashed off.

CHAPTER 4

S OMETHING ABOUT THE way Charles had said that made Emmeline smile. She wasn't sure about his earlier invitation—whether it was as one friend to another friend or something else. Her mind was just confused and adrenalized enough with everything going on here that she didn't dare put any credence in the words because—in dire situations like these—people said and did all kinds of things that they regretted later. She didn't want to be somebody who did the same. As she barreled into the servants' kitchen, she met Terkel. "We have one," she said, gasping for breath.

"One what?"

"Intruder."

At that, Terk bolted to his feet and asked, "Where is he?"

"Downstairs, the basement level. Charles is holding a gun on him. We tied him up, and we knocked him out. Well, Charles did, then I did too." She explained as they raced downstairs, Wade following, who looked at her in surprise.

"Hey"—she managed a laugh, even as they ran— "Charles and I are old hands at this."

"So I've heard," Wade said, with a head shake. "I thought you guys would have been farmed out of the service a long time ago."

"When they decide you're no longer prime for active duty, you go into intelligence to keep things running in the background," she murmured, humor in her tone.

"Better not let Charles hear that you think he's old," Terk warned them, with a grin.

"Good Lord, no. I don't think he's old, but obviously he's no longer as quick as he was twenty years ago," Emmeline added.

"I think," Terk noted, "that Charles would say, *Thank heavens for that because with age comes wisdom*, and God knows we could all hope for more of that." Terk came to a running stop in the basement to see Charles, indeed, standing guard, but, as they arrived, he held up a finger for silence. Terkel stepped up and checked the guy on the ground to see if he was still alive. He took a picture of his face and then moved closer to Charles. "What's going on?" he whispered.

"They argued, and his partner bailed. We're afraid he'll come back in this tunnel, as a way to hide from everybody out searching the grounds."

"That's possible," Terk murmured. He pulled out his weapon. "You stay here. I'll go down." And, with that, he headed deeper into the tunnel.

AS TERKEL RACED quietly through the tunnel, he sent out a telepathic alert to the rest of the team. It might be a bit garbled because of the concrete tunnel, he assumed, but he wasn't sure that something else wasn't going on here too. At least they had Bill, the one escapee they were looking for. The fact that he'd come with a partner wasn't exactly a surprise, but the fact that the partner might have left him was interesting. But, with Terk's people hunting the intruders outside, it would have been easier and safer for the guy's partner to stay underground and to wait for the commotion to die down and then sneak back outside again later.

Up ahead, Terk saw footprints in the accumulated dirt and dust, but he didn't have enough light to discern where anyone had gone. However, being in a tunnel, he wouldn't have used a flashlight anyway. It would only give away his position. He did have his parasenses and saw a fresh energy signature. He went past a side tunnel and then stopped and slowly backed up because the tunnel definitely broke off and went up in a different direction.

Sending out another message to his team, he quickly changed directions, then seeing fresh tracks heading along this new route, he followed them. As the tunnel shifted upward and around a corner, he started to curse this old place. They really needed to map it out and quickly, before anybody else found this too.

As he came to the end of the tunnel, he thought he heard a commotion up ahead, and his footsteps stilled. As he followed the energy, he thought he might be under the small servants' kitchen. As he stepped into another room that appeared to be more like cold storage, he realized that he was literally right under the smaller kitchen now. He entered slowly, his senses attuned, but he couldn't see anything physically. Yet a faint energy trail headed to a small door at his side. It was short, low enough that he would have to duck to go through it. He was excited to get this secret tunnel all mapped out because, as far as escape routes went, this would be huge.

However, as far as having intruders enter without him

and his team even knowing about it, that was a problem to be dealt with immediately. With his eyes closed, he mentally counted energies, and then he stopped, frowning.

He was getting multiple energies, and he knew the women would be up there because that's where he'd ordered them all to go. Including Celia and his babies. It did appear that an intruder was in the mix. Studying the energy around what should be the intruder, Terk frowned, then reached for the door handle. There was just too much energy flowing in that room. Could be fear. Could be anger. Quietly pulling the door ever-so-slightly toward him, he opened it and stepped through. Now he was in a small empty room. A storage room.

This room he had been in before—the pantry to the servants' kitchen—and the next door Terk should find would lead directly into that kitchen. Moving as silently as he could, he headed closer to the kitchen, and there he heard voices.

"I don't care what you think you should do," a stranger snapped. "I told you to get over there. All of you, on the one side of the room. Take the little boy with you."

At that, Terkel frowned. No way in hell he would let anything happen to his people in the kitchen. And Little Calum was there as well. And, even at that, he heard Calum Sr. in his head, sounding the alarm. Terk sent back a reassuring note, as much as he could because he still didn't know what the scenario was. From the sounds of the voices talking, it was only the one man, and that in itself was interesting because it also aligned with what Charles had said. Terk got closer and heard more.

"No. We won't move anywhere. You really don't want to be doing this," Clary warned in a hard tone.

Terk winced at that because now this guy had no idea how close to death he really was.

"I'll do whatever the fuck I want to do. I'm the one with the gun. Remember that?"

She laughed. "You might have a gun, but, if you think that we're without weapons, you're wrong."

There was a moment of ugly silence. "All right, put your weapons on the table, and that's enough out of you. I'm not taking any bloody chances. I know my buddy was after somebody here but also money. Big money was here. Now I want to know what the hell was so important that you would risk getting killed over."

"I have no idea." Clary got up. Terkel could tell by the sound of the chair going back.

"What are you doing?" the gunman asked.

"You told me to put all the weapons on the table," she murmured in a joking voice.

"You think I'm being funny?"

"No, and I don't know what you're up to, except you have no idea what the hell will happen to you when the others find out that you're in here."

"If they didn't want uninvited guests, they should have closed the damn door then, shouldn't they?"

"Pretty sure they will now." Clary laughed. "At least as soon as they get two minutes. Having just moved in, it's a case of not enough time to sort everything out."

"A lot of people would have had the sense to take care of business before they ever moved in, except for guys like you. What the hell? Don't have another place to stay or something?"

"No, we didn't. … Aren't you tired of holding that thing? Isn't it getting heavy?"

"No, it's not getting heavy. When my buddy talked to me about some woo-woo stuff here, I thought he was pretty damn crazy, but, just in case he wasn't, don't you even think about trying any of that with me."

That was as close to the truth as Terkel even wanted to consider that this guy knew, and Terk was grateful that this guy still didn't seem to really understand anything. He was just shooting questions in the dark.

"Woo-woo stuff?" Cara asked in a curious voice. "What on earth would that even be?"

"I don't know," he snapped in frustration. "Same as I don't know why it was so important that he come in here and finish this job. Something about a big payout."

"If it's the payout for a contract killing, I can tell you right now," Mariana spoke up, "the guy who would pay you is dead."

A long silence came. "*Contract killing?*" he asked. "Nah, my buddy's stupid but not that stupid."

"He may just be stupid enough not to realize that the contract was rescinded because nobody is paying for it."

"I don't believe you. I don't believe any of this. You must have some valuables in here somewhere."

Clary picked up the conversation again. "Maybe somewhere but we haven't even unpacked yet. So I don't even know what to tell you about that. But how about this? It's just you against what? Ten of us here? Not to mention our partners."

"I don't know how many there are, but you're making me nervous. So get the hell away from that table and go over to the corner. I can't even believe that you're trying to pull something here. I've got a gun for crying out loud."

The trouble was, nobody seemed to be respecting his

gun, and Terk could already see how dangerous this was getting because, depending on the gunman's temperament, this guy might just open fire and start shooting everybody around him. And the danger of that would include Little Calum and Terk's unborn twins. Terk wasn't sure just how far Little Calum's abilities would extend when it came to firepower. Just as he took another step forward, Clary spoke up again.

"I really would put down that gun, if I were you," she snapped. "You won't like what comes next."

CELIA STARED AT the gunman. "You see? Nothing here is what you expect, and nothing here will happen the way you think it'll happen," she murmured. "So I would strongly suggest that you just back away, kindly crawl into whatever hole you came from, before it's too late for you."

"What the hell do you mean, too late for me? I'll go down there and double-check on my buddy but not until I make damn sure that all of you guys are tied up so you can't come after me. And then, when I find him, we'll go through this place with a fine-tooth comb. We'll take everybody down and haul out everything we can carry. Hell, we might even bring a team in here," he boasted, with confidence. "There's got to be loads of stuffs here we can steal."

"Ah, so that's what you're after, whatever nickel-and-dime stuff you can steal, *huh*?" Celia asked, and then she laughed.

Almost instantly he exploded into fury. "Don't you fucking laugh at me," he cried out. "You don't know anything about me."

"I know that you are trying to make a few bucks off a job and that you have no idea what kind of hellish situation you've put yourself in."

"Why is that?" he asked.

She looked up to see Terkel, his gaze narrowing, as he studied the room from around the corner. She sent him a quick telepathic warning, but it was obvious that he already knew what the danger was.

"I don't know what you're talking about," the gunman glared at her. "Maybe you should explain it."

"Explain what?" she asked, then deliberately moved an energy shot to the glass on the table in front of him. When it skidded off table and fell to the floor and crashed, he jumped back and screamed. She looked at him and gave him a flat smile. "Yeah, that sounded like a real big macho man scream, didn't it?" Celia asked the others.

Clary laughed. "I always love how men seem to think that women are completely helpless and need some big badass stranger to swoop in to look after them—or, like in your case, one against ten, and you just think you'll take us down because we supposedly don't have anything to offer in terms of a fight." She shook her head. "Buddy, consider her advice and take a hike."

"What happened to that glass?" he asked, but now his voice wavered in panic.

"What glass?" Celia asked, and this time Clary sent one skidding off the table to crash on the floor.

"Jesus," he cried out, "are there fucking ghosts in this house?"

"You know what they say about these old buildings," Clary replied. "They hide all the ancestors who have gone before."

"No, no, no. Ghosts are not real." The gunman shook his head, staring at them wanly. "You guys are just messing with my head. These are tricks, like with ropes and things around here somewhere. I don't know, but there has to be."

"Oh yeah? So we saw you coming, and we set it up as a show?" Celia snorted.

"What the hell? I should just take you prisoner. You're pregnant, so you'll be the easiest one to take down."

"Absolutely not," she drawled, "but you're welcome to try, if you really think you're that lucky."

He stared at her. "I don't get it. Why are you not even scared?"

"Scared of what?" Celia looked at him with amusement. She found it to be a pretty damn strange scenario to be in, but absolutely nothing inside her told her that she needed to be afraid of this guy. Maybe it was coming into her own power. Maybe it was the power of the babies surging within her womb—her mama bear instincts overriding any others—but, for some reason, she had absolutely no fear of the gunman. Of course, knowing that Terk was right here was helpful too. She smiled at the gunman. "Are you sure you don't want to just take a hike right now? To save yourself?"

He glared at her and waved the gun in her face. "Do I have to shoot somebody to make you people realize how serious this is?" he roared. "That's fine. I will."

"What?" Cara stood and took a step closer to the gunman. "Seriously? That's how you think you'll control a group of women? You'll shoot one of us, and we'll all break down and cry, then do everything you say? What'll happen when we all jump you? You certainly can't shoot us all at once."

He looked nervously around and took a step backward, right where Terk waited. The gunman shook his head.

"Look. I don't want to hurt anybody. Honestly I just need something to cover my costs, so I can get the hell out of here."

"Oh, so now you're just looking for a quick payoff?" Celia asked, laughing. "I can't take anything you say seriously. Not to mention the fact that you just threatened my unborn child, so, as far as I'm concerned, we should just deep-six you into one of the old forgotten wells on the property." She sneered at him. "Nobody will ever know."

He stared at her, and she realized that he was starting to believe that something here was terribly wrong.

"You wouldn't do that," he said nervously.

"You're the one waving a gun at my face, threatening my baby and all my friends here." Celia took a step closer, until she stood right beside Cara. "We gave you the opportunity to leave, unharmed, and you haven't, and that's a problem." Celia stuck out her hand. "I suggest you hand over that gun. We won't kill you if you behave, and, if you're lucky, neither will all our men, when they get here."

He swallowed at that and took another step back. "See? They can't do that. I'm just trying to get out of the situation. I had planned to just leave, but people are outside searching, so I couldn't go that route. I had to come back inside."

"Yeah, and where is your friend?"

"I don't know," he cried out, visibly shaking now. "I didn't hear any gun shots though."

"Yeah, well, nobody told us that we have to use gunpower in order to take out our enemy. Just like that glass, we could break you where you stand."

He started to cry out, "No, no, no, you don't have to do that."

"Then put down that gun," Celia murmured, "and you

give in right now and stop with your stupid petty thefts and threats. Then we'll bring the men in to take care of you."

"What? So now you need the men to take care of me?" He perked up again, trying for a more macho look.

"We don't need the men to deal with you," Cara said, her voice deadly, "but the men will want to know about this little display of yours."

"They won't care because my friend is taking out the ones who need to be taken out, and I still think you're lying about the contract killing. He'd never do something like that. I mean, theft is one thing"—he waved his hand—"but murder? That's just beyond him."

"It's not beyond him. Do you not realize Bill escaped from MI6 for that very thing? Plus, he was involved with international criminals, who are on the wanted list for Interpol," Celia explained, with a smile. "And then of course the CIA out of the US wants to talk with him as well, just as soon as they get the chance."

"No, no, no. He wouldn't have gotten mixed up in something that stupid."

"Maybe you should take a moment and rethink things going on here, before you get yourself into trouble that you will pay for with the rest of your life. Assuming you survive today."

"I don't know." He glared at her. "This is all ridiculous."

It was obvious that he didn't know which way to go or how to get out of the situation he had gotten himself into.

Celia almost felt sorry for him. "Tell you what. Why don't you start by putting down the gun, so nobody thinks you're still actively trying to shoot us. Then you can turn around and return the way you came," she suggested, with a bright smile.

He looked at her hesitantly, took another step back. "But, if I put down the gun," he stated, "I won't have any weapon. … And I still don't understand why you're acting this way." He seemed completely perplexed.

"No, of course not, but you also don't know what we know."

"What's that?"

"That there's no way you'll get out of here alive, as long as you keep that gun in your hand. You might get out on your own if you leave now, but, as soon as the men come back, which I can already hear is happening, you'll be out of options."

He stared at her, looked at the door behind her, looked back at her, looking like he wanted to bolt.

"You can run," she called out, as he backed out some more, "but you can't hide."

"The hell I can't," he cried out, "and you won't ever see me again."

"I wouldn't count on that. That's presuming you get out of here safe and sound and in one piece."

"Of course I am." And he took another step back. "You don't seem to be as scared of the gun as you should be, and I don't really want to go down as the guy who shot unarmed women in their own home. And I don't want anything to do with Bill, if he is involved in contract killing. Yet I still think you're wrong, and I've got to give him a chance to show me."

"Right," she said, fascinated. "So, what will you do?"

"I'll leave and talk to him later."

"Yeah, you do that." She beamed at him. "That's presuming we don't already have Bill in custody."

"Do you?" he asked.

"That's for you to find out, isn't it? Or you could just leave and see if he ever shows up again. And that would be your answer too."

He stared at her, moistened his lips, nervously looking from one to the other. Obviously he was completely over his head and didn't have a clue how to handle this situation.

"I'll just leave. Sorry for disturbing you, ladies."

"Yeah, no problem," Clara said in a hard voice. "Make sure you don't make that mistake again."

He shook his head, spun around, and ran. Right into Terk's fist.

Terk looked around the room. "Everybody okay?"

All of them nodded.

"We're fine." Celia smiled, as she walked toward him, and flung her arms around his neck. "I suggest you get this shit fixed real fast."

He groaned, wrapped his arms around her close, and murmured, "Believe me. I'm trying."

"Try harder," she whispered.

He chuckled. "It sounded like you all had this well in hand."

"It'll be a cold day in hell before any of us will let an asshole like that take away the bright future we have planned. I've also decided," Celia declared, "that I don't want these babies to be born without a father."

He looked at her in confusion, as the other women started to chuckle. "I'm confused," he said. "I am their daddy."

"Absolutely you are," she murmured. "But you're *daddy*, not legally the *father*."

He shook his head. "There's a difference?"

"A difference that matters to me, yes." She took a deep breath. "I want us to be married." She pulled her arms tighter around his neck and kissed him gently.

"So give me a moment to just clarify this," he said. "Are you telling me or asking me?"

The other women burst into laughter.

Celia chuckled. "I'm not getting down on one knee, and, as much as I consider myself a modern woman, I still would prefer to be asked. However, given our unique situation, I guess the question really is, *Will you marry me?*" He wrapped his arms around her, picked her up, and gently swung her around in a big circle. "If you'd given me a chance, I was planning to ask you."

"Apparently you're too slow." She grinned down at him, still in his arms.

He burst out laughing.

"Okay," Celia said, "now how about an answer?"

"I have an answer for you. How about a screaming loud *yes?*" Then he lowered his head and kissed her, right in front of everyone.

CHAPTER 5

EMMELINE LOOKED OVER at Charles, who smiled at the group in a benevolent manner. He was thoroughly enjoying himself.

"I might need your help to pull off this wedding," she murmured.

He chuckled. "I doubt it, but my help is always available."

She smiled up at him. "Somehow I'd forgotten how nice you were."

He looked at her in surprise and then shrugged. "I'm the same as I always was."

"Not so sure about that. I saw you only as my husband's friend for the longest time." She shrugged. "Then I slowly started to recognize just what a good man you were, all on your own."

"I'm glad you finally made that distinction." Charles chuckled. "I'd hate to think I was still living in his memory."

"No, not at all," she said warmly. "It's just odd to realize how much the passage of time has changed things and to see how differently things can appear."

Charles noted such an odd reflective tone in her voice that her words probably even surprised even her.

She added, "He seems to be on my mind lately."

At that, Charles patted her hand. "I think that's where

they're supposed to be," he reassured her calmly. "When you think about it, we don't really want to forget about them."

"No, but it's been over a year," she murmured.

"So, is it time you moved on?"

"He would say so, absolutely. But move on to what? Just when I think I have moved on, then I'm not so sure."

"And why worry about it? Just live each day, knowing there's always a chance that it could be your last, and I'm sure you'll do fine."

She chuckled. "Most people would not find any peace looking at life that way."

"I know, but, after you've been in danger more than a few times or experienced random and traumatic loss, you realize that it really is something that could happen on any given day. So you need to do something to protect yourself as much as you can and yet live each day to the fullest."

"Agreed," she murmured. With some of the hilarity ebbing around her, Emmeline turned to Celia. "And when you say *soon*, how soon do you mean?"

Celia faced Emmeline. "The babies are taking more out of me than I expected. And I don't know that they won't make themselves known a little earlier than planned."

"You could just tell them to stay in there and to behave themselves," Clary suggested.

Celia looked at her and laughed. "Do you think I haven't tried?" The two women grinned.

Because everybody knew there was that bond already, between parent and child.

"Honestly," Celia added, "I didn't think that being pregnant and not married would bother me, but I feel like so much was already taken from me, from us, over this scenario, that being married isn't something I particularly want to let go of."

"And there's no need to," Terkel said. "We'll get the job done."

She looked over at him, a smile on her face. "Could we think about it a little less like a job on the to-do list?"

He chuckled. "Now that's why somebody else needs to handle the arrangements," he admitted, "because I'll go at it with military precision, and I'm not sure the end result will be what you had hoped."

"As long as we're married at the end, I'll be fine." Celia grinned. "Besides, these kids will come no matter what, so, in a way, it doesn't really make a difference"—she shrugged—"yet in some ways it does matter. It matters a lot."

"If it feels like it's something important, then we need to do it," Charles spoke up. "So, depending on whether you have any particular wishes for how you want this done—"

Celia immediately shook her head. "No, I don't. I don't want a big formal affair. I don't want anything other than the friends and families we have here, more or less. If there are a few more people to invite, then I'm all for that," she offered, "but, if it needs to be less, that's fine too. I really just want to have that process taken care of."

"We should discuss it a little more. I can probably arrange everything for you, if you're comfortable with that," Emmeline murmured.

At that, Celia looked at her with delight. "Do you think so?"

"Probably, as long as you're not expecting too much. Because it will take some time, plus the location might be booked out, so you need to settle on a time frame. Are we talking three months, one month, or one week?"

"One week," she said instantly.

At that, Terkel sucked in his breath and looked over at Emmeline. "Can you even manage that?"

She nodded. "I can manage it, as long as your expectations are in line with that time limitation."

"I feel like you're hedging your bets on that," Celia said, with a grin on her face.

"We'll have to look into the local legalities of course. I don't believe it needs to be in church, although it can be, and a church does provide for a lovely setting. Do you have a preference?"

"There is a small church just around the corner," Charles said. "I've seen it driving in. It looks quite lovely."

"The church it is, then a simple reception here after the ceremony?" Emmeline probed further.

"That all sounds wonderful." Celia sighed happily. "And again, nothing too fancy, just us."

"Not a problem. I can certainly handle that." Emmeline looked over at Terkel. "If you want to invite other people, perhaps you could handle that?"

He nodded. "Probably a few, depending on how Celia feels about it all. Those who are already here could potentially be enough though."

"I'll leave room for say another four to six people, and, if it'll be more, please advise. I'm sure I can rope Charles into giving me a hand with this." She looked over at Charles, who immediately nodded.

"With pleasure," he beamed. "I do love a good wedding."

She laughed. "I remember. As I recall, you are also one to cry at weddings."

"Not if I can help it," he protested, "but they are definitely something I am partial to."

"In that case," Celia said, "I am more than happy to leave all this in your capable hands." She sighed. "Frankly it's a little bit out of my element, and I feel like, between now and then, all I'll do is sleep."

"If that's how you're feeling," Terk said, "then that's what you should do, particularly if those babies are looking to arrive early."

"I hope not. Anything short of thirty-six weeks can be problematic."

"So, in that case," Terkel murmured, "you need to lie down, relax, and talk them into staying put."

She winced. "I get that. I really do. It just feels like they have a mind of their own."

At that, Clary stepped forward. "I might be able to help with that."

Celia looked at her hopefully. "Really?"

Clary nodded. "But I have to go in and talk to them."

Emmeline stared, fascinated by the whole thing.

"Can you do that?" Celia asked in astonishment. "As in, more than I talked to them?"

"Yes." Clary nodded. "However, it wouldn't be a conversation as you would typically think of it."

"No, of course not," Celia muttered. "It's not as if they can talk back."

"Oh, they'll talk back but not the way you would expect," Clary said, chuckling. "All these babies have a mind of their own anyway, and your body does too. It's got a time frame and an agenda, so, depending on how things work, we'll see what we can do. I can't guarantee that I can hold them off, but one thing I do know is, the less stress on you, the better."

At that, Celia frowned. "Please don't tell me that I have to stay in bed for the next month or something."

"Nope, not in bed," she clarified, "but maybe sitting with your feet up to alleviate some of the strain on your body, while everybody else does some running around, looking after you for a change. We can always prop up a laptop on a pillow for you or something."

"I'm really not so good at sitting around. And I sure don't want to cause anybody extra work."

"I don't think that's really an issue now," Terk noted calmly. "And there is plenty of work you can do for this company. But, for now, the babies have to come first."

"Right." She looked down at her enormous belly. "Honestly I'm still adjusting to the fact that we're even in this condition."

"You and me both." Terk chuckled, shaking his head. "You and me both."

At that instant, the doorbell rang. Terk looked over at Charles, with an eyebrow raised.

The older man immediately nodded. "Yes, I highly suspect that will be MI6."

"*Great.*" Terk groaned. "Too bad they already know where we live."

"That is unfortunate, though it was only a matter of time. But, at least in this case, they owe you." Charles rubbed his hands together in delight.

"We do have their missing prisoner," Terk muttered, thinking again of how badly that all could have gone. As he walked toward the front door, along with Charles, Damon wasn't far behind them. "You ready for this?" Terk asked Damon.

"Never when it comes to these guys," Damon said, "but

it's not as if we have a whole lot of choice."

With that, Terk opened the door to find Jonas and two other men with him. Jonas glared at him.

"Hey, we caught him for you." Terkel glared at Jonas before he had a chance to open his mouth. "So maybe don't lose him this time."

"We didn't lose him that time," he blustered. Then he frowned, seeing Charles there. "Okay, fine. So we lost him. But we won't lose him again. Where is he?"

"You mean *them*." Terk tilted his head. "He apparently hired somebody to come help out."

"Of course he did," Jonas muttered. And, with that, Terk led him down to the prisoners, where Gage and Wade sat close by on watch. As Damon stepped aside so Jonas could see, the two prisoners started accusing Terkel's team of abuse and kidnapping.

Jonas just growled at them. "Stuff it, you two. Nobody wants to hear it." And one by one, they eventually shut up. He motioned at the two men behind him to collect the prisoners.

Bill spoke up. "I really would prefer not to be in this position."

Jonas growled. "You two got yourselves into this mess, so, as far as I'm concerned, we can throw away the key."

"Except we do have some information for you."

"Yeah, what's that?"

"How about the name of the guy who has the contract on Terkel here."

"The dead guy?" Terk asked.

"Nope. The current guy, who was picking it up as an extra tidbit because you guys offed his buddy."

"Yeah, and what's his name?"

"Roger," he said.

"I don't know any Roger." Terk tried to appear uninterested.

"No? Well, you should know Roger's brother," Bill said. "He was one of the guys killed in all this, and now Roger has murderous intentions where you guys are concerned."

"We didn't do anything but defend ourselves," Terkel said, with a shrug. "Roger's brother was the idiot who hooked up with the asshole who put out the original contract."

"But it is still your problem in that they're coming after you. It's not my fault this guy decided to pick up the contract. I mean, it's pennies compared to what the original contract was, but it's what the guy could afford."

"You've got the name, so I presume you've got the contact information as well," Terk stated.

The guy nodded. "I do, but I want something for it."

"I'm sure you do." Jonas shook his head. "Come on. Let's get him back to the jail." He grabbed the arm of the second man, who now glared at Jonas and his buddy who got him in this mess.

"I didn't have anything to do with this, so I hid inside. That's it. I didn't do nothing."

"On the contrary"—Celia stepped into the room next to Terk—"that is a lie. You pulled a gun on a roomful of women and a young child. You threatened us and, in fact, were looking to steal whatever you could get your hands on."

"Hey, I had to get money somehow," he protested. "But my way was nothing compared to what Bill was planning to do to get paid."

"I didn't do nothing either," Bill cried out, and, still wrangling, Jonas's men led them out of the house.

"You may have escaped once," noted an MI6 agent, "but we won't let that happen again."

Terkel followed them out, Charles at his side, listening in and trying to make sense of this new twist. "You need to find out who the hell it is that still has a contract on me," Terk said calmly to Jonas.

"Chances are, the prisoner's just lying, trying to make something up to get himself out of this," Jonas argued. "They are lowlifes who don't know anything."

"Maybe, maybe not"—Terk nodded—"but I can't say that I'm particularly fond of the idea of somebody else having a contract."

"You should be getting used to it. I would think, for you guys, it would almost be a usual thing."

"Maybe so, but that doesn't mean I like it."

Jonas snorted. "And I'm supposed to care, why?"

"You're supposed to care because otherwise it'll come back on you," Terk stated carefully. "You keep us safe, then we keep you safe."

"Except we're MI6."

"Yeah, we don't exactly have a name yet, but don't worry. We will, and then you'll know exactly who you're dealing with, if you don't already."

"I have a pretty good idea who I'm dealing with," he snorted, "and are you sure I can't convince you to return to the US?"

"No. This will be home. Right here."

"Here?" Jonas asked, looking at the old estate and frowning. "Holy crap, the private industry gig must be going really well."

"It's phenomenal." Terk grinned.

"So now we have Bullard over in Africa, Levi in the US,

and you guys over here. That's just great."

"On the other hand," Charles said, with a bright smile, trying to ease some of the tension with a gesture of goodwill, "there'll be a wedding soon, and you're invited. Terkel and Celia are getting married in one week's time, and you, of course, are invited. We'll send you an invitation with the details."

Jonas stared at him, nonplussed.

Charles gave him a genuine smile. "It probably would be a good idea," he added, with a small smile.

"You do know my bosses would not approve, right?"

"On the contrary, my lad. Your bosses will approve when they realize that it's good business relations."

"Are you sure the wife-to-be will be happy with these *good relations*?" Jonas asked.

At that, Celia stepped forward and patted her belly. "The wife-to-be will be quite happy to have you come to the wedding, assuming you'll leave your scowl behind and you'll bring the kind and gentle version of you," she said, with a bright smile. "And, hey, let's just hope we get the wedding done before the babies show up."

Jonas looked at her large belly and took half a step back in alarm.

"You really don't want to mess with a pregnant woman," she said softly, but definitely a threat was in her voice. "Like it or not, we have moved into the neighborhood, and we're staying. This will be a perfect place to raise our children."

"And the industry?" Jonas asked, staring at her. "It's a mess out there."

"It's a mess everywhere," she declared. "And, if we're guided by fear all the time, we won't get anywhere as a society. So come or don't. Either way, you are welcome. As

Charles said, invitations will be coming out soon enough."
She chuckled. "I promise I won't go into labor during the
wedding."

"I don't know." Jonas grimaced. "That's looking pretty … ominous."

"It is, and there are twins involved. So, of course, we
want to get married first."

"Sounds like a good idea." After a slight pause and a big
sigh, he looked over at Terkel. "We need to talk."

"We do, indeed," Terk acknowledged with a nod. "Give
us a chance to get set up, and we'll get some meetings
planned."

"And you'll stay out of trouble in the meantime?"

"Listen. As long as everybody's taken care of who tried to
blow us up in France and now here, and we don't have
anybody else coming around after us, it'll be fine. But I have
no guarantees of that yet from you."

"No, I don't either," Jonas said, "but I'm hoping." And,
with that, Jonas took off with his men and the prisoners.

Celia turned to look at Terk. "Do you think that's the
end of it?"

"I'm not sure," he murmured. "We'd like to think so,
but we'll stay extra vigilant for a while, until we sort this out.
By rights, this guy shouldn't have been here at all."

"I wondered that myself. And he hired somebody to
come with him. I wanted to get married and quickly for the
babies," she explained, "but there's definitely another sense
of urgency." He looked at her in alarm, but she shook her
head and laughed. "No, the babies aren't on their way."

"Darn good thing. They're much better off inside."

"I know, but it feels like I won't do very much but sit in
bed in these upcoming days."

"No, you probably won't. And I think the idea of a lap-top with your feet up is likely as much activity as you'll handle."

"That's kind of a depressing thought. I've always been very active."

"And now you're carrying two very active children," he murmured, holding her close. "Come on. Let's get you to bed. You and the twins need to make an early night of it. There's been way too much excitement around here."

"I'm hardly that delicate," she protested.

"It's got nothing to do with your delicacy at all," he said, wiping his brow in an exaggerated motion, "it's mine." She burst out laughing at that and was still chuckling as he led her upstairs to their room, where she quickly got ready and curled up under the covers. "Are you coming, too?" she asked drowsily.

"Not just yet." He sat down beside her on the bed. "We have to seal up the new tunnel we found today. I don't want any more surprise visitors getting inside."

"I know," she murmured. "I'm thinking that, when I wake up, I'll hit those figures and the cost analysis from Emmeline. I really don't know how we would have done this without her."

"All of it shouldn't have fallen on your shoulders, that's for sure, but I appreciate your efforts. We definitely have a lot to handle, and we're trying to do an awful lot at once."

"I know. It almost feels like maybe too much all at once," she said, yawning, "except I can't see how we could stop what we're doing and focus on something else."

"That's the problem. We need a fully functioning com-pound. Everything needs to be done at once, and it's all interrelated. Sounds like Emmeline's sending in another team of a whole bunch of people tomorrow."

"Good," Celia said, with more spirit than she felt. "We definitely need them," she murmured. And, with that, she yawned once again.

Terk leaned over and gave her a gentle kiss on the cheek and murmured, "Good night."

TERK GOT UP and walked out to the bedroom doorway, staring down at her. To think how quickly his life had changed was mind-boggling. And now a wedding coming up next week was also amazing and pretty unbelievable. As he walked back into the kitchen and poured himself a cup of coffee, the others looked up at him expectantly. "I know. We need to have a meeting. We need to do some planning on the security here, and we need a discussion about what the hell just happened."

Charles nodded.

"And I thought you were leaving too," Terk said, looking at him.

"I think maybe I'll stay here tonight, if that's okay. I would leave, but then, with so much going on, I could be right back here tomorrow. So might be better if I stuck around for a while."

"Are you sure you're okay with that?"

"Of course I am." Charles shrugged. "Obviously things here need to be prioritized, and we must get moving on as many of these issues as we can."

And, with that, Terk nodded, brought up his notepads and launched into a discussion on the outside perimeter security. Nobody wanted to hire an outside defense company, but, at the same time, they needed help—at least until their compound was fully functional.

At that, Levi suggested, "I can involve Bullard, if you want. He would get a kick out of this too."

"Is he the best person for the job? What about you?" Terkel asked, staring at him.

"This is bigger than my place," Levi admitted, "and Bullard helped with securing my compound as well. Plus, I'm already helping on the inside, and there's only so much I can do."

"It's okay with me, if Bullard is willing," Terk replied. "We'd discussed it before. I just didn't know if it was really necessary, but we've bitten off quite a bit here."

"Ya think?" Chuckling, Levi pulled out his phone and quickly placed a Zoom call. When Bullard answered, Levi grinned at him in greeting.

"What's going on?" Bullard asked. "Sounds like you guys are having fun somewhere without me." His voice boomed across the place.

"That's true enough," Levi replied, "and we've just had another incident tonight, so we really need to get the security system in place here." Then he quickly explained about the intruders.

At that, Bullard's face creased in concern. "That's not good. You've got to get that shit set up fast."

"I know, so, even if you could help guide us from afar on some of it, it would be great."

He thought about it, his fingers churning. "I wish I could just come on over."

"We're not asking you to do that," Levi stated. "I know perfectly well how you feel about being there for the birth of your baby, and we've got the same problem here with Terk.

He's getting married next week and is about to have twins."

"Twins? Now isn't that something." Bullard grinned, shaking his head. "I thought one was scary. We'll all be overrun with babies, won't we? Our wives will have to open day cares in each of our compounds."

Levi nodded, with a knowing smile.

"You're not the first one to mention that," Terk said, his tone gloomy. "It does something to our image though."

"Screw the image, man," Bullard snorted. "We have a life now, a real and full life, and that's worth so much more. Listen. Send me the blueprints, and I'll check Google Maps too. I'll send a team over and a bunch of supplies." Bullard chuckled. "We'll have a private jet coming your way soon." He thought about it, then continued. "I don't know if I can get them there tomorrow. It will probably be the next morning. Let's set up some kind of a plan tonight, so I get the layout there, and we'll start shuffling things your way. Then we'll send a follow-up set of supplies in a couple weeks."

"Any way to make that a couple days?" Levi asked. "This place is huge."

"Give me an idea of what you're dealing with," Bullard said.

"Hey there, Terkel here." He stepped into Bullard's view. "We've got twenty-two acres. The main building itself is four stories aboveground, plus an additional two underground. Then a farm area is included, with barns and all kinds of other outbuildings. We've only now just discovered some tunnels that weren't on the blueprints, so we'll have to investigate further immediately. That's how two intruders got in."

"Damn, you really bought a castle, *huh?*"

"I did," Terk stated. "It has a name, though I'd have to look it up somewhere. Anyway it'll be quite the place when we get it done."

"It will be," Bullard declared. "It sounds amazing. Don't worry. We'll all help ensure it's safe. Nobody needs to lose any friends or family when it comes to this crap. We're all in the same industry, and not a one of us would turn our backs on the others."

"Thanks, we really appreciate it," Terk said. "One of these times, we'll have to visit again."

And, with that, Bullard called over one of his IT guys, and they all settled down via Zoom into discussions about what kind of security system Terk needed and who would install it. By the time Bullard hung up, quite a lot of time had passed, and Terkel looked over at Levi.

"That is a huge load he's bringing," Levi said, shaking his head.

"He meant it about the jet too," Terk said in a calm voice.

But Levi's fingers were rattling away on the desk.

"What's the problem?" Terk asked.

"No problem, it's just that there's still so much to deal with, and a big one is you guys don't have your own satellite. You need that."

Terkel looked at him with a frown. "No, and our budget doesn't include the ability to get one just yet either. We've got to get this other stuff finished and the final numbers in before I could consider that."

"It is one of the big expenses that you'll need to figure out and fast."

"And how the hell are we supposed to do that, when there's so much other stuff to fix at the same time?" Terk tapped the notepad in front of him. "We've got to get the basics dealt with."

"No, I hear you," Levi said. "Let's get started and see what we can knock off the list." For the next hour they went over room by room, all that they had sorted out for particular inclusion into the security system—the armory, the gym, and the jail. At that, Terkel looked over at him. "Oh, crap, what about a medical room?"

"You'll definitely need one of those. And be sure to ask Ice to tell you how to outfit it."

"That would be a huge help if she could. Or Bullard too for that matter," Terk muttered.

"Yeah, he and his wife. She's a doctor."

"Everything in its own time. Let's at least get a room designated for that purpose first."

Levi thought about it, then pulled the blueprints toward him. "It would make sense that it would be somewhere around here." He pointed. "You'll have to get those big service elevators in, so you can get stretchers or a gurney through here," he muttered. "But, if you have access from the outbuildings, that'll be where you bail out anybody who needs to be driven in. Do you need a helipad?" He paused to think about it, and that brought up even more discussion on other topics too.

By the time Terk looked down at his watch, another four hours had passed. "Wow, it's late. I feel like we need to crash now, then come back with some fresh brain cells in the morning," he muttered. "Once Bullard's team gets here, we'll have to sort through and deal with a ton more."

"There'll be more than a ton." Levi laughed. "But, by the same token, he'll have the ideas that we need to make this work."

"I hope so." Terk hadn't been all that worried about money, until they started talking about things like elevators and satellites, and he realized just how big a project he'd taken on. He looked over at Levi, as the others started to get up. "Just ballpark, how much money are we talking for a satellite?"

The others stopped and looked over at him.

"Millions," Levi said quietly. "No way to get around it though."

"Jesus. Fine, that will give us something to aspire to."

"It took us quite a few years to get there," Levi shared, "but it is the *one* thing that we use constantly."

"We would too. And we're used to having access to that kind of equipment, when working with the government." He groaned. "We're just not used to figuring out how to pay for it."

"No, of course not," Levi said, "but the fact of the matter is, when it's necessary, it has to be done." And, with that, they called it a night.

Terk headed off to bed, his mind full, as he sorted through everything they had discussed. As he lay here in bed, Celia tucked up against him.

She murmured, "Go to sleep, honey. Your mind is making too much noise."

Chuckling, he slowly shut it down, curled up next to her, and crashed.

CHAPTER 6

W HEN EMMELINE WOKE up very early the next
morning, she bounded out of bed and headed to the
servants' kitchen. She put on coffee, made herself a quick
breakfast, then sat down at the table with her checklist. She
needed to get a handle on some of these things, figure out all
the phone calls that needed to be made, who among this
special group she could put work on to, and what she needed
to hire someone to take on.

But, at the same time, Emmeline needed to pass off a
bunch of this money stuff to Celia to take over. That girl
needed to stay off her feet as it was, and now they had a
wedding to arrange. Emmeline frowned, as she thought
about that. If she could give a lot of that wedding planning
over to Charles, it would help. But he might not want to
take that on. She couldn't really blame him, since he was
busy doing security stuff, which is something he excelled at,
so asking him to take on a wedding was definitely not the
easiest or the most natural shift.

For her, it would be fun. It's just she had a time frame
issue, but she'd promised to get it done, so she would. That's
just the way life was. As she continued to work on her list
and nibbled away on her toast, others slowly came to join
her. She looked up as each one walked in, smiled at them,
and went back to her work.

Celia sat down beside her. "What are you working on?"

"Lots of different lists," she said, taking a sip of coffee. "I'm basically doing a brain dump at this point, listing things that need to be done today, people I need to phone today, and things that we'll add to our work list for the wedding to happen."

"I kind of feel bad about that." Celia winced. "You're already dealing with so much."

"So, I'm dealing with a little bit more," she said cheerfully. "It's really not an issue."

"I do like that, thank you very much," she murmured. "Your attitude is very refreshing."

Emmeline just smiled at her. "You have a job right now, whether it's what you ever thought you would be doing or not. Your job is to do your very best to bring those babies safely to term."

"That point has been brought home to me a few times now."

"I'm sure it has," she said, with a smile, "and you can expect more of that as you get closer."

She nodded. "So, have you got something for me to go work on?" Celia asked.

"I do. I figured that, after you've had your breakfast, you could head up to your room, where we'll get you set up with a laptop. With your feet up," she added. "Do you think I haven't noticed that your ankles are starting to swell?"

She winced. "Maybe don't pass around that detail," Celia whispered.

"Too late," Clary said, as she walked in. "I'll do some energy work on you today and see if we can get that to stop."

"That'll be great if you can"—Emmeline stared at Clary thoughtfully—"but I sure don't know how you'll manage it."

Celia giggled. "You have no idea."

And, with that, Emmeline realized that these women probably had even more skills then she'd ever seen before.

"I'm up for trying anything you've got to make this easier," Celia told Clary, with a grateful smile.

"Not sure how it'll work, but I don't see why it wouldn't." Clary shrugged. "I've been dealing with all kinds of issues and cases over the years, so we'll come up with something. If not, my sister's here, and, between us, surely we can do something."

"I hope so," Celia murmured, "and thank you."

And, with that, Emmeline got up and gathered her things. "I'll head over to the office and put some things together. I'll be up to your room in what? An hour?"

"An hour would be good," Celia said cheerfully. "I'll probably be ready to put my feet up by then anyway."

Nodding, Emmeline headed for the room she currently thought of as her office. Her head was full of figures and numbers and lists, some that she needed to rewrite for added clarity before she passed them on to Celia. As Emmeline made her way there, a bunch of workmen stood in the front hallway, waiting for attention.

"Good morning, who is it you're waiting for?" Immediately they gave her a name, and she nodded.

"You're early, so I'll take that as a good sign." From that moment on, she was crazy busy. By the time she turned around, several hours had already gone by, and she had yet to sit down and finalize the information for Celia.

Focusing on getting that done, she was soon ready and walked up to Celia's room and knocked on the door. When she stepped inside moments later, she apologized immediately. "I'm so sorry. I got waylaid by a crew that showed up a bit early, and one thing led to another, and I've only just now come up for air."

Celia laughed. "I think that's the way it's likely to go for quite a while."

Emmeline nodded. "You're probably right. And that's all good, as long as things are moving forward."

"I did see a bunch of men in the front hall earlier."

Emmeline nodded. "A veritable smorgasbord of tradesmen and not a moment too soon. Everything from plumbers and electricians to carpenters and masons, but, of course, that also meant that I had to go get them each settled on their various assignments." At that, she handed over a big stack of pages to Celia. "I finally did find time to rewrite a few of these lists," she said. "I hope it's self-explanatory, but you know where to find me if you have questions."

"Yeah, I know where to find you all right." Celia laughed. "Going crazy."

"Maybe a bit." She smiled. "But it's all good, and we'll get to the bottom of these projects pretty fast," she said. "We just need to get started." And, with that, she turned. Then pivoted. "Before I forget, tell Terk that all those boxes in the tunnel last night are filled with antiques. I have yet to inventory and price them. Just tell him it should easily cover these initial setup costs."

And she walked out.

CELIA SMILED, AS she shared that good news with Terk via their special telepathic link. That should settle him down some where the budget and their account stood.

Now she stared at the paperwork in front of her and

then brought up the calculator on her laptop. By the time lunch had rolled around, she was amazed at how much work was getting done here, as evidenced by all these invoices. The figures were shocking to her but maybe not so much, considering how much sheer work was involved, how much had already been achieved, with probably a rush fee involved. Regardless it was all important. And now they seemed to have antiques to pay it all off. *Amazing.*

She got out of bed and headed down to the servants' kitchen, where everybody was coming and going, looking for food. As she walked in, Mariana looked up and smiled.

"How's the pregnant lady?" she asked Celia.

"Feeling kind of pregnant at the moment," she muttered. "Any chance of food?"

"Lots of leftovers in the fridge."

"That would be perfect. I'll just warm up a plate then. Anything off-limits?"

"Only if it's marked as such. I learned that the hard way early on with this bunch."

Celia pulled some things from the refrigerator and settled into warming up a plate of food. When she turned around, Terk had come into the kitchen, looking for her.

"I'm right here, just getting something to eat." He looked at the mound of food on her plate, and his eyebrows shot up. She shrugged. "Don't you dare say a word." He slowly closed his mouth, while Mariana laughed at him.

"Good save there, Terk. A very smart move, indeed."

"I'm learning." He grinned. "Believe me. I'm learning." Terk faced Celia. "I understand we have a potential windfall coming by way of antiques in this place. That's good. I won't worry so much about the expenses then. And I got your message that you had a bunch of cost overruns and some analysis to go over? Even with our windfall, we want to try to stick to our budget, if possible."

"Yep," she said, "I brought it with me, just in case, so I've got it all right here. If you want to grab a seat, we can go over this while I eat." With that, he grabbed a coffee, and the two of them sat down. "It took me a while to get my mind wrapped around the size of these figures, but, once I got through what it all meant in terms of services and goods, I felt better."

"Good to hear."

And, with that, she got started.

Terk shook his head. "Some of these figures seem pretty darn high for me too. I'm used to running big operations, and the costs are what the costs are, but when it's coming out of our bank accounts, and still so much more is left to do, it's a little on the scary side."

"Even if we have to wait several months for the antiques to be sold and money deposited in our account, I think we'll be just fine. I did take a peek at the bank statement," she said drily.

He looked at her. "You think so?"

She nodded. "Absolutely, but we'll have to keep an eye on it, just to make sure things don't go crazy."

"You mean like a satellite crazy?"

She frowned, as she looked over at Mariana, then back to Terkel. "If you tell me that's something that you need to keep us all safe, then it's no longer a potential acquisition to consider but a necessity, and it moves up the list."

"It's not a higher priority than finishing the repairs," he noted, "but it would definitely be on the wish list."

"And you're still not telling me what I need to know."

He hesitated, then sighed. "I've had access to them

104

through all my working life, and they're definitely an advantage. For the moment, we can probably get help from Levi and Ice, utilizing their satellites."

"But ideally we need our own—is that what you're saying?"

He nodded.

"Fine." She rubbed her temples, as she thought about the cost of something like that. "I presume we're talking one million plus?"

"According to Levi, yes. And that's also not exactly something that you can just pick up ready to use. It has to be ordered, and delivery can take time. Not only that," he added, "we have to get somebody to launch it into space for us."

Her jaw opened slowly and then closed. "Fine, I don't even want to know. I presume between Levi and Bullard that they know who to contact because they've already done it once."

"Exactly." Terk grinned.

As she watched him, it was like seeing a little boy take over his future. "Aside from money worries, you're really having fun, aren't you?" she said, chuckling.

"Hey, with the security system planning we've been doing, it's like toys for big boys," he declared, with a smile. "Almost anyone would enjoy this."

"Maybe. I'm just glad you're having some fun." And, with that, she went into some of the more detailed progress discussions that she'd had with Emmeline.

"Good enough. It's easy to physically see what isn't done and focus on that, but by going through these records, it shows me that things look to be taking shape and are coming along nicely. This list really helps to focus on the big picture," he said, looking over at the master list that Emmeline had put up on a big chalkboard. The lines struck through so many different items were impressive. "The fact that she's even getting a chance to take something off that monster list is amazing to me because it seems like it's never-ending."

"I think she feels that way too," Celia agreed, smiling. "There's obviously been progress, and that's something we can all be grateful for." He agreed with that and very quickly he was up and gone again.

She shook her head at the speed at which her life had changed. As she sat here, apparently staring off into space in some kind of an altered state, Mariana walked over and sat down beside her.

"Celia, maybe it's time to go have a nap, *huh?*" she asked, as she gave her shoulder a gentle shake.

"What? Did I look like I was zoning out already or something?"

"You not only looked like you would zone out, you *were* zoning out."

She sighed. "There's just so much going on. It's exhausting just being here."

"It's exhausting just being pregnant, and you've got twins, so I don't think that being here is necessarily the problem."

"No," she murmured, "it probably isn't." As she looked over at Mariana, she asked, "Would anybody mind or think it was weird if I headed off to bed?"

"No, I think they'd mind if you didn't," she murmured.

Taking that as a yes, Celia got up and headed off to get some rest. "Tell everybody I've gone to have a nap."

"Will do, and don't come back until you're ready."

So, with the paperwork in hand, she took it up to her room and crashed. That last thought on her mind before she dozed off was that she hadn't seen anything about the wedding. Not a list, not an overrun, not a cost analysis, nothing at all. She worried about it for all of one minute, then realized she was just too damn tired to think about it. She closed her eyes and immediately drifted off to sleep.

BY THE END of the day, Terk was done in so many ways. Though it had been a good day, he was tired and frustrated at some of the security questions they needed to answer but didn't know how. That was the thing that got to him the most. There were decisions that needed to be made, but they were waiting now on Bullard's team to get here before they started committing to things in the security system that they might have to change later. It was one thing to tackle a job solo and to get it done, but it was another thing entirely to start a collective job, make a decision, and then have to redo it all because something changed. Just as he was about to say something to Levi about it, his phone rang. "Hello, Jonas. What do you want?" Terk asked, putting it on Speaker.

"And here I thought we were better friends than that," he replied in a disgruntled tone.

"Have you got something good for me?"

"Not really. The second guy has been let go."

"Well, hell, if there was ever a reason to not set up here in England, your lack of law enforcement might be it."

"My investigators say that he was cooperating, was hired just for this one job, and doesn't know anything about the upper-level organization."

"Sure he's cooperating, and I agree that he probably had very little if anything at all to do with any of this at the beginning, but that doesn't mean he isn't seeing a paycheck at the end of the day, doesn't mean he won't break in to steal from us later, doesn't mean he won't be here again, pointing a gun at my pregnant fiancée or at my team member's son."

"He was rambling on, something about that damn woman."

At that, Terkel stiffened and slowly looked at the others. "Right, the one who faced him down?"

"Yeah, I guess, although it sounds like they all had him rattled because they weren't afraid of the gun. Anyhow, this is a friendly warning call. I'm not sure what she or they did to piss him off, but there is a chance that he's holding a grudge."

"Great, and you guys let this guy go."

"I didn't," he protested, "but the locals declined to prosecute. How are the wedding plans going?"

"Honestly, I don't have a freaking clue," Terk murmured into the phone. "It's all I can do to keep my head straight on everything else going on right now."

"No wonder, that place will be a bear to get into shape. But, once it's done, man, you'll have an incredible setup."

"I hope so, but I might be calling on you for work."

Jonas snorted at that. "Asking us for work is one thing, though hopefully we won't have anything going on that we'd need you for. But keeping out of trouble would go a long way to further your cause, if some potential work did come up."

Terk huffed. "I hear you, but I don't think you hear you because, so far, we've been overrun doing your work."

"Yeah, I do remind the higher-ups of that, but they're

not too interested in hearing it anymore."

"Of course not. Listen. Thanks for the update. I really appreciate it, and we'll talk later. I've got a million things going on here."

"Did I hear that Bullard's coming to town?"

"Wow," Terk murmured. "Why would you have heard that?"

"Ah, so he is then. Make sure he stops in and says hi."

"Last I knew, he wasn't coming himself, but he is sending over a team to help us set up our security system."

"Oh, I don't know about that. That may not be a good idea."

"Doesn't matter if it is or not," Terk stated, frustrated. "It is what it is at this point."

"Bullard's been known to push the line."

"Of course he has. We all have. We don't really have a choice sometimes."

"I know that. I'm just saying that, if he does turn up, it would be good if he stopped in. As a courtesy, you know?"

"I'll pass it along," Terk said, then ended the call with an eye roll toward Levi, who nodded.

"Honestly, Jonas is on our side a lot," Levi noted, "so anything you can do to make it easier on him would be smart."

"I get it," Terkel said in frustration, "but pussyfooting around with a government has never been a forte of mine."

"Well, short of letting one of the women handle it, you or somebody in this outfit better get good at it because there's really no other way to handle these guys."

On that note, Terk glared at his friend. "You know that's bullshit, right?"

Levi nodded. "Absolutely it's bullshit, but these guys we

deal with have bosses, and, if we can keep our contact person out of their boss's crosshairs, our contact will be much more likely to help out. At the end of the day, we have to deal with it, and they hold an awful lot of the cards, you know?"

"Yeah, I know," he muttered. He looked around at the rooms being cleaned top to bottom. "I do have to admit. Things are starting to take shape."

"When the cleaning is done to that basement area, we still have all the boxes that need to be gone through," Levi reminded him.

"Yeah, I'll let Emmeline go through them first and catalog everything, and then we can figure out what's here."

"That's not a bad idea," Levi murmured.

"It's a brilliant idea because she has an eye for antiques. If I let the guys down here, we'd probably end up throwing out the good stuff."

"Jesus, could you see Wade down there or Rick? They'd make quick work of it, *huh*?"

"Yeah, and the next thing you know, the local trash man will be retired and buying himself his own island paradise or something." They shared a good laugh at that, something Terkel really needed. "If we find anything valuable, it will get immediately sold because that satellite needs to happen."

At that, Levi chuckled. "Yeah, that's kind of how we felt about it too. I didn't realize it at the time, but Ice had been putting money away for years, trying to get the satellite. Then we took on one big job, so we could get the rest of the money for the satellite."

It was all an eye-opener to Terkel. "I've done a lot, but this is kind of like that next step."

"It absolutely is," Levi said. "And it would be good if you had somebody with a business background or at least the ability to learn it quickly."

"Yes, it would be. I'm not sure how Celia would feel about it, but she's really smart and has a lot of business sense."

"I wouldn't worry about it right now. She's got a lot on her plate," he murmured.

"You think?" Terk quipped, shaking his head. "We're all making a lot of adjustments right now. I'm pretty happy about how well everyone is getting on and working together. Everybody is keeping busy at something."

"I know," Levi said, with a happy smile. "Things are working out pretty well, huh?"

Terk smiled. "I really should have expected that though."

"Expected what?"

"How the way things that are meant to be just fall into place. Like all these partners and the whole twin thing," he pointed out. "Merk and I of course being twins, then Katina and Celia both carrying twins." Terk had said it without a thought.

However, Merk, sitting nearby, spewed his coffee, then slowly turned and looked at him. "What did you just say?"

Terk's eyebrows raised, as he looked at his brother. "You didn't know?"

"Ah, no, I didn't know, and maybe the better question is, *Does Katina know?*"

At that, Terkel winced. "Not sure she does. *Oops.*"

Levi started to laugh and laugh. "Oh my God, that's rich. That kills me. Wait until Ice hears. She'll be over the moon. Jesus, we'll need a day care center at our place soon. Hey, Merk, buddy, are you okay?"

"*Twins.*" Merk turned yet another shade paler.

"Yeah, well, how do you think I feel?" Terk said to his brother. "You at least had the fun of creating them." At that, all of them burst out laughing.

"There is that." Levi turned serious and asked Terk, "Will you have more children?"

"Hey, I'm the last person to be making predictions on anything like that." Terk frowned. "It's plenty challenging enough to get through what we're doing right now."

"Got it," Levi said, but Merk still looked shell-shocked.

"Do I even mention it to her?" Merk asked the guys.

"I wouldn't," Levi said immediately. "That's her domain."

"Yeah, but I can't be dishonest—"

"You can tell her, but it may not make her very happy," Terk noted.

"Oh, good Lord." Merk scrubbed his face. "I think I better go call and see how my wife is."

"You do that," Levi said, still chuckling.

Then Merk stopped, looked at his brother, and asked, "You're sure about this, right, bro?"

"I'm sure, man. Sorry. I didn't mean to spill the beans."

"No, with you, it's always that way." Merk shook his head and quickly disappeared.

Levi looked at Terk and smiled. "You definitely like to shake things up, don't you?"

"Honestly, I rarely even think about these things," he replied. "Something comes into my head, and then it just pops out. It can get me in a hell of a lot of trouble."

"I can see that, and I can see why." Levi nodded. "Finding out you'll be a dad from somebody else is one thing, but finding out your wife's carrying twins and chances are she doesn't even know about it, that's a whole different story."

"Yeah, and that brings up another point," Terk said, as he looked around at the men starting to filter in.

"What's that?" Levi asked curiously.

But Terk frowned, looked over at Levi and, with a small headshake, told him it wasn't a conversation he wanted to continue just then. Levi studied him for a long moment, then suddenly looked around, his eyes widening, and a grin formed on his face that was hard to contain. But Terkel hoped that Levi would keep down his mirth, until a discussion was had with these guys later, before it became something they would all have to deal with after the fact.

Just then Terk's phone rang again. He looked down at his screen and answered, "Hey, Jonas. Now what?"

"We have somebody from Bullard's team asking permission to enter the country," he snapped. "They're bringing a crap load of equipment, but they don't have a proper manifest."

"You know exactly what it is. I told you already."

"They still need to bring in the proper paperwork."

"So tell them what paperwork they need," Terk said, with an eye roll.

"Yeah, well, Bullard's not being terribly cooperative. He wants us to just let them in."

"And you have a problem with that?"

"I'm trying to keep my job," he muttered.

"The easiest way is to let them in, with a warning. All that stuff's coming here so we can try and get the security set up, so we don't have any more of your prisoners running wild and out of control after they escape from your custody."

"Hey, hey, now," Jonas growled. "Be nice."

"I'm trying to be," Terk muttered, "but you guys make it difficult."

"Fine, I'll talk to them again and see what kind of paperwork we can arrange here." And, with that, he hung up.

"Did he really need to call us about that?" Terk muttered.

"Not at all," Levi said. "That was just his way of saying, 'Hey, this stuff is coming at you. I know it's coming. Just make sure you don't screw us over.'"

"If that's all it is"—Terk huffed—"I'm sure he'll handle it just fine in the end."

"I don't think he has any intention of handling anything. I think he's feeling a little pissed off that you guys are setting up shop on his turf," Levi stated, with a big smile.

"Maybe, but damn," Terk muttered. "We obviously have to get used to having some relatively important visitors."

"But don't treat them like that," Levi warned him. "They do like it, but it's not a good habit to get into. Because one day you'll forget, and they'll wonder what happened."

"Right."

Just then Emmeline walked in, plunked down a load of paperwork and said, "Whew, I need coffee."

"How about food instead?" Levi asked, studying her. "You're looking a little peaked."

"*Food?*" she questioned, as if he'd just mentioned something completely foreign. "That's probably not a bad idea. I was up and running early this morning, but now, if you can believe it, we've got twenty-seven workmen on the job today alone." She gave him a big fat smile.

Levi whistled. "I do like to see people working. Maybe you can come back and get my place shipshape when you're done here."

At that, Terkel snorted. "Your place is shipshape already. Ice is a wiz at handling that, and, what she doesn't cover, the rest of your clan does."

"That's true, and it's pretty amazing how well everything runs. You'll get there before you know it, Terk," Levi murmured. "It'll just take a little time."

"It will take time," Emmeline agreed, "but not as much as we first thought."

"That's good news."

She walked over to the kitchen and said, "Mariana, I know it's your domain here, but can I make myself a sandwich out of something?"

"Actually it is sandwiches for lunch anyway, and it's time. So, if you want to call in the rest of the crew, we can get started." With that, Mariana brought out platters and platters of make-it-yourself sandwich ingredients.

And Terkel could only stare, realizing that Alfred had Bailey over at Levi's place. "What about staffing?" he asked Emmeline, as he reached for bread and fillings for a sandwich.

"Just tell me what you want."

He looked over at Mariana. "What do you want for the kitchen in terms of staffing?"

"I don't want to cook seven days a week, all day long," she said. "And I'm not sure whether everybody here wants to take turns cooking, or hire somebody."

"I vote we hire somebody," Clary said immediately. "I can't cook worth a crap." She laughed. "So the days that I'm supposed to help out, you'll all be sneaking off and ordering takeout."

Terkel grinned at her. "Can't be that bad," he teased. "Look at that. You make a wicked sandwich." He pointed at her plate.

"Only because I've had so much practice because the rest of what I'm not so good at."

"Maybe a better question," Cara asked calmly, "is how many people are you planning on keeping here and for how long?"

Terk looked at her, frowning. "What do you mean?"

"Are you expanding your team, or is this as large as you're getting?"

"Oh," he said, "I see myself expanding."

With a twinkle in her eye, she asked, "Do you plan to expand with more interesting people, like us, or will you go with the more mundane types?" She sent a teasing sideways glance back and forth at Levi.

Levi rolled his eyes. "I don't know where he found any of you to begin with"—Levi shook his head—"but his growth should be a whole lot slower just because of that. And it'll take a whole lot more time for you guys to integrate," he murmured. "So doing anything quickly won't be helpful."

"No, it won't," Terkel agreed, "but I figure that we'll need things like weapons specialists, more admin assistants, a bookkeeper, and all that. We'll need people for added security quite possibly. And honestly, if we branch out to doing missions to pay for things like a satellite, we'll need more men."

"Just men?" Levi asked. "Don't forget Sophia," he said, with an arched look. "She's the real deal."

"Nope, absolutely not just men," Terk confirmed. "So, Emmeline, if you know any men or women with the same skill set, let me know."

"But it's the other part of that skill set that I don't know how to source," Emmeline said, "and, like Levi, I can't imagine that you can get very many people who do what you do."

"You'd be surprised," Celia said, as she walked in and sat down beside Terkel. She rubbed her belly, while she stared at the table in front of them with joy. "Ooh, sandwiches."

"Yeah, you're pregnant and hungry." Levi chuckled. "Ice was a bottomless pit. Every time we turned around, she would have both fists full of food."

Merk snickered, as he walked back into the kitchen. "I remember that. It was crazy." With a knowing look at his brother, he added, "If you're right, she doesn't know it."

"I'm right."

At that, Merk's shoulders slumped. "I don't even know what to say about that." He reached for a plate and some bread.

"What did I miss?" Celia asked.

Merk groaned. "According to Terkel, my wife is currently carrying twins as well."

She looked at Merk, frowned, tilted her head, and then nodded. "Boys."

Merk stopped, stared. "What the hell?"

"*Oops*," she winced, looking back at Terkel. "I guess that wasn't fair, was it?"

But Terk was chuckling. "My brother should be used to me doing that, but he's worried about saying anything to his wife."

"Merk, I'm really sorry," Celia apologized. "Things just pop out of my mouth before I even have chance to think."

"God, you two are so alike that you're just scary." Mark snorted. "And, if you're right, well, … damn."

"It should be a good damn," Terk noted, with a smile.

"I know, and it is." Merk smiled. "And, honest to God, you're the best brother a guy could ever have."

"I just try to keep you safe," Terk replied cheerfully.

"Yeah, you do at that." Merk looked over at Celia. "Damn, sons." And he finally started to grin. He looked over at Levi. "The guys will be pissing in their pants when they find out."

"I know. I can't wait." Levi chuckled, then turned back to Terk. "And when will you mention anything about the numbers in this place?"

"I thought that was part of the discussion we would have now," Terk said, "but then I saw Mariana there, working so hard, and started talking about hiring more kitchen staff instead."

"What do you mean?" Tasha asked.

He looked at her and winced, as she stared at him. "What did I say?" Terk asked. At that, everybody looked at him, and he groaned, as he looked over at Celia and then at Clary. "I don't know what I said. Do you want to give me a little help here?"

Clary looked at him and around the room. Then it hit her. Her grin started, then got wider and wider. "Oh my God," she cried out. She looked back at Celia, who stared at her, not really comprehending. Then as she looked around the room, it was as if an electric bulb hit her as well.

Just then Cara got it as well. "Are you kidding?" Cara said. "Is it infectious or what?" She bolted upright, her hands going to her own belly. Clary looked at her, Celia, and around the room.

"Is everybody here right now?" Clary asked. They counted heads, and everyone was there, including Emmeline and Charles.

"So, do you want to explain this?" Tasha demanded. "You're starting to scare me."

"Not necessarily but, as we're talking about staffing plans," Terkel said slowly, "I don't even know if this is a thing anymore, but what about a midwife?"

Immediately everybody looked over at Celia.

She tried hard to keep her grin back. "So, one of the problems with being around pregnant people is that it heightens my psychic abilities because I can get energies from these guys inside, but it also makes something else a little bit contagious too."

"What the hell does that mean?" Gage stared at her in shock.

"It means, I'm not the only pregnant person in this room," Celia said in a rush.

CHAPTER 7

EMMELINE STARED IN shock, as she studied everybody's face one at a time.

But Charles, with his twinkling gaze, spoke next. "I don't have to be psychic to know a couple of them. I was wondering if people really hadn't been clued in yet."

"They really haven't," Clary said calmly. Then looked over at her sister. "Or did you just now?"

"I did just now." Cara laughed in delight. "My God."

"I know, right? Not exactly where we thought we'd find ourselves."

"You two are pregnant?" Rick and Brody exchanged a frown, looking from one to the other, then to the other set of twins in the house, Cara and Clary.

Clary winced. "We both are pregnant, yes," she confirmed. Then she took a deep breath, looked over at Wade and Sophia. "So are you two."

The look on Wade's face had Emmeline laughing out loud. "Oh my." Emmeline asked, "Is it really because all of you have so many different abilities?"

Terkel nodded slowly. "It makes fertilization that much stronger. The energy builds and grows so fast when we're together like this, and we'll all notice a lot of changes in a lot of areas." He shook his head. "And although birth control may have been utilized in some of these cases," he noted, "the body has a way to get around everything."

Wade just stared, and then he turned to look at Sophia in shock.

Sophia also stared at everybody and cried out, "Oh, no. No, no, no. No way I'm jumping on board the pregnancy train, and no way you can force me."

Celia gently said, "No force required. I'd say you're about eight weeks along."

At that, she gasped. "What?" As she counted back and looked over at Wade. "That would be near the beginning of our relationship."

"Yep." Wade stared at her and then back at the others. "Are you guys sure?"

"Oh, yeah," Terkel said. "The thing is, you aren't the only ones."

Complete shock reverberated throughout the room.

"We can't set up a team if everybody'll be pregnant," Gage cried out. "What are we, a reproductive team? Or a security team?"

"And, in your case, you might not be," Celia said.

"Might not, as in you can't tell if we are, or we just aren't?"

"No," Celia said calmly, "not that I can tell at the moment. But at least four of us are right now, and the other children coming will just be younger." A silent sense of shock filled the room, until Charles broke in with a shout.

"I, for one, am delighted," he said, beaming. "Children are such a blessing."

"They're also better when they're planned," Tasha whispered, almost numbly.

"You did plan it, my dear," Charles said. "And that baby responded. For whatever reason, these children all needed to be born right now."

"God," Tasha said in shock. "What a way to find out."

"I don't think the way you learn of it has anything to do with it," Celia said earnestly. "And at least you already know that you love and care for your partner."

Tasha nodded slowly. "I know, but wow. This is like so public."

"Yeah, tell me about it," Celia teased.

At that, Tasha winced. "Lord, Celia, I'm so sorry for what you went through. As disorienting as this is, it's not a fraction of what you must have felt. And you missed out on a lot, didn't you?"

"I did, but I also gained a lot," she said, with a gentle smile. "So, in the end, it all worked out."

"I guess." Tasha looked shell-shocked. "I'm still a bit bewildered over the whole thing."

"And that is to be expected," Celia stated. Then she stopped, looked at Tasha. "So, do you want to know what the sex of the child is?"

Tasha opened her mouth and closed it about three times in a row, then slowly she shook her head. "I don't think I do."

"Good, then I'll do my best not to tell you." She winced and said, "But it's possible that it might just pop out."

"It might," Clary agreed.

Tasha looked at Clary and asked her, "Can you tell too?"

She nodded. "Both my sister and I are carrying girls."

"One or twins?"

She looked over at her sister and raised an eyebrow. "What are you getting?"

"I know I'm carrying twins," Cara said calmly. "What about you?"

"I'm carrying twins, too, so it's four girls. And you two are having boys."

At that, Terkel nodded slowly. "We are, that's four to two." He looked over at Levi. "You weren't kidding about a day care, Levi. And I wasn't kidding about a midwife. And a nursery, family apartments or even wings," he added, as an afterthought. "Apartments in different wings might be a good idea. Family life, a bit of privacy, yet communal. Good God, we need to think and think fast before we start making plans on how we'll keep all of this in-house."

"In-house?" Tasha stood up slowly, her hands on her belly. "I think I need to go lie down and adjust to some rather unexpected news."

As she stumbled away, Damon gave everybody an odd look and said, "I think I'll go spend a few minutes with Tasha," and he disappeared too.

Terkel looked over at Celia. "Will they be okay?"

"They will," she said. "It's just a bit of a shock when you first find out, and, finding out this way, it's that much harder. But they'll be fine," she murmured, with a big smile. "Just think. Our babies will have friends."

CHAPTER 8

E MMELINE WOKE UP the next morning, still reeling from the revelations of the day before. Charles promptly took her aside, and they talked about what had gone on last night. She stared at him in shocked delight. "My God," she whispered, "I wonder if any of them realized their special energy was doing that?"

"No, I don't think anyone realized anything until yesterday," he admitted. "But obviously some safeguards will have to be put into place for it not to continue, at least not more than they wish it to."

She snorted. "And yet we also know how good Mother Nature is at making things happen her way."

He nodded slowly. "Isn't that the truth? Anyway, I wouldn't bring it up at this point, but it's definitely a consideration now for your calculations as to the living quarters herein."

"It's more than a consideration," she said, her mind spinning. "We need to take a fresh look at this floorplan. Some of these rooms need to be reconsidered in terms of playrooms, nurseries even, depending on how they want to do it."

"So, what did we end up with so far? It's Tasha, Sophia, Cara, Clary, and Merk's wife, right? Like wow. So the dads are Damon, Wade, Rick, Brody, and Merk, is it?" He nodded. "So eight babies, with three sets of twins that we know of there."

Emmeline shook her head. "I've got to focus on the work now." Still stunned at the change of events, she quickly turned her attention back to what all needed to be done because now it was even more urgent to get it finished and in working order.

Not too long afterward she had another thought that stopped her in her tracks. She quickly tracked Charles down and asked for a moment.

He walked away from his conversation with Terk. "What's the matter?"

She took a deep breath. "Given what we know about the impending births," she asked, "is this wedding likely to get much bigger?"

Staring at her in surprise, he turned and looked around at everybody, only to turn back and face her. "I have no idea," he whispered, "but I guess it's possible. It would make sense, wouldn't it?"

"Well, it might," she said, "but they may not be ready. As I understand it, most of these relationships are fairly new."

"Yes," Charles agreed, "except for Mariana and Calum, who married years earlier, I believe. Though Damon and Tasha worked together for years, they both avoided the obvious attraction and pushed things back for another day."

"And we see what happened with that plan," she said, with an eyebrow waggle and a chuckle.

"Isn't that the truth," Charles murmured, still stunned at the issue she had raised. "I don't even know who to ask at this point."

"I was wondering the same thing. But, if plans are

changing and if we're expanding this wedding ceremony, I kind of need to know. It could expand the guest list in a big way, not to mention the reception."

"Or we just do the one right now." He stopped and looked around. "Who do we even approach to ask?"

"Celia, she's the initial bride."

"Yet she's the newest member of the group and doesn't know the others that well."

"Right." Emmeline frowned. "I have no idea then. I mean, who is it we should be talking to?"

"Terk," Charles said immediately, spying him ahead.

Hearing his name mentioned, he turned and looked at them, then raised an eyebrow and walked over. "Problems?"

"We're not sure whether it's a problem or not," she said calmly. "But having heard about the increases in family size coming up"—she hesitated, trying to state it as delicately as she could—"I'm just wondering, and you'll have to forgive me because I don't even know if this is something I should be bringing up."

He just waved her on. "Go ahead, pretty much everything is up for a team discussion right now. We're all still reeling with the news."

"Except you, I presume."

"I'm still trying to adjust to being a father in the first place. And getting married, since Celia wants to get married before the babies were born."

"Considering now a lot of other babies are coming ..." Emmeline began again, as he looked at her for a long moment, still not comprehending, and she realized she would have to just bite the bullet and say it. "I'm wondering how many of those other women will want to get married too?"

He stopped, stared, and said, "Oh."

She laughed. "It would be easier to consolidate all of them into one wedding, though I'm not saying that needs to be what happens. But, if that was what someone wanted to do, I'll need to know fairly soon. Bottom line, I'm just wondering if any of the other couples want to get married at the same time as you and Celia."

"Oh, wow." He sat back on his heels and stared at the two of them. "I haven't the slightest idea."

"If you don't know"—she grinned—"does anybody know?"

"God, I don't even quite know how to approach it." Terk seemed completely sidelined by her words.

"And I get that," she said. "I really do, but we are having one wedding, and everybody will be there."

"So, therefore," Terk surmised, "it would be an expedient way to do it."

"Yet, if you put it that way to the women involved," Charles noted on a laugh, "the response is bound to be unpleasant."

Terkel winced. "Right, because it sounds like we're doing this more out of convenience and timing than anything else."

"Exactly. So I'm not sure what to do," Emmeline added.

"*Great*," Terk muttered. "And here I thought the day was going so well."

"It is," she said cheerfully. "I mean, I couldn't be more thrilled."

He looked at her with a wry smile. "Yeah, how do you feel about being a godmother or grandmother? We are a little short on outside family."

"Is everybody here short on outside family?" she asked.

"More or less, for one reason or another. Hopefully now this next generation might help with that," he said, "but it won't be an instant type of healing."

"No, of course not. I never thought of that. I guess the abilities can make things difficult, can't they?"

"More than difficult," he noted. "For a lot of us, it's like a final straw. In some cases, people won't believe that it's a real ability at all, thinking it's just a case of people making up crap. And eventually that becomes unforgiveable for almost everyone."

"Wow," Emmeline murmured, "I hadn't considered that."

"No, of course not. And part of our problem with the abilities is the fact that there's really not a whole lot we can do but accept them and work with them. They are what they are, a part of us, like it or not. But when families don't believe or accept, it just becomes that much more complicated."

"How very sad," she said.

He nodded. "Sad, yet at the same time, freeing—because, once we're free of the unbelieving family members, it does become easier for us to open up our own abilities."

"I guess so. I just hadn't considered that it would break up a family."

"The things that break up families are pretty amazing. At the same time, Merk and I have no extended family anymore. It's just the two of us, and, without him in my life, I would have found it very barren."

"All the more because you're twins, I'd imagine," Emmeline agreed.

"Exactly." Nodding toward Clary and Cara, he continued. "No family member wanted anything to do with them either, and these delightful twins were given up for adoption when they were quite young, along with their brother, who is deceased. Whether that was because of their abilities starting to manifest or something else, we don't know, but neither of them has any family that they know of and none that they can sense."

"And that makes a difference too because, if they can't sense family, what are the chances of there being any?"

He nodded. "Precisely."

"So, are we bringing this up with the four pregnant women, or am I just to continue down the pathway of the current plan and hope that you guys don't suddenly, out of the blue, decide that all these arrangements need to expand in a big way at the last minute?"

"Crap." Then Terk looked around. "I guess a meeting with the twins might be the best way to start."

"I'll leave that up to you then," she said, with a genuine smile.

Terk looked at her and glared. "You're the one who would be in a better position to do this. After all, you're the one making the arrangements."

Charles nodded. "I hate to say it, my dear, but he's right."

She looked over at him in surprise. "You aren't throwing me under the bus, are you?"

He chuckled out loud. "No, that wasn't my intention at all."

"But …" she said.

Charles heard the *but* loud and clear. He just smiled. "I am wondering if we shouldn't get Celia's take on the matter before we raise it with anyone else."

"How so?" Emmeline asked.

"Maybe she wants this wedding just for herself. We don't want to take the sparkle out of her special day."

"That's a really good point," she stared at Charles. "I should have thought of that myself."

"I highly doubt it would be an issue for her," Terkel said. "But I agree, we should find that out first."

Emmeline nodded. "Fine, I'll talk to Celia about it as soon as I can."

And, with that, Terk nodded in obvious relief, then bolted.

She glared at Charles. "That was hardly fair."

"Maybe not but you are the right person for the job."

With a groan, she rolled her eyes at him. "Says you."

He took a few steps closer, then engulfed her in a big hug and said, "I have the utmost faith in you."

She sighed, as she nuzzled in close. "I'm glad you do." Then she chuckled. "I mean, what could be worse than pregnant women getting married?" she asked, with an eye roll.

At that he chuckled, stepped back, and said, "Go on now. Go for it."

Spying Celia up ahead, Emmeline made a beeline toward her. "Hey, can I have a moment?"

"Absolutely you can. I was going to track you down myself today."

"Good." They grabbed some tea and headed to one of the empty rooms. "Now," Emmeline said, as they sat down. "You probably want to talk about business, right?"

"Yes," Celia agreed. "I was also trying to avoid any wedding talk."

"Oh." Emmeline stared at Celia, only slightly flummoxed. Soldiering on, Emmeline asked, "Any particular reason?"

"I don't know what I want. I don't know what I should have, what's appropriate. I don't know anything about it. And honestly, I don't want to make this sound like it's just something to be expedient about, since it is supposed to be a sacred ceremony, but, in some ways, I just want to get it taken care of so I can enjoy the rest of my pregnancy without worrying about it."

"I can understand that." Emmeline frowned, wondering how she was supposed to proceed now.

"Oh dear." Celia winced. "I presume from the look on your face that you have wedding questions."

"Something has occurred to me, and, yes, it's wedding related. I just don't know if you want this wedding to be focused on just you and be super special or—"

At that, Celia looked at her and frowned. "Or what? Is there an alternative?"

Emmeline lowered her voice, leaned forward, and murmured, "It occurred to me that now that we know there are several other pregnancies happening, I wondered if there might be others interested in getting married at the same time, given the fact that we would have everything ready and probably a similar guest list and all. I mean, obviously it's more complicated to have multiple couples at once, but it's definitely easier than arranging multiple separate weddings. Particularly with everything else that's going on."

Celia looked at her in shocked surprise. "The thought never occurred to me." And then she clapped her hands together. "From my perspective, that would be perfect, and it would make all of this a lot easier on me."

"How do you figure that?" Emmeline asked, with a raised eyebrow.

"Because I feel bad about the expense and all the fuss. So much else needs to be done here—though, I know, if I brought up the cost of the wedding, Terk would get after me."

"Of course he would. It is a celebration."

"But considering that it's not just me getting married, it would also remove the spotlight that frankly I'm not all that comfortable with." She was definitely warming to the idea.

"Maybe we should discuss it with the others?" Emmeline suggested. "Though I don't even know that discussing it with them is the right answer. I don't know how everybody else is likely to feel about getting married, and I don't want to be pushing people's buttons."

"Oh, I think they're already pushed." Celia frowned. "I'm not sure that we did a great job announcing it to everyone like that yesterday. We were worried about telling them, but, at the same time, it is something that needed to be known by all for the sake of security, if nothing else."

"I don't think there would ever be an easy time to give the team that information, as you said to be fully informed." Emmeline smiled. "So you really didn't have a whole lot of options."

"Exactly. But, at the same time, I feel that maybe we took something away from people, and that was not our intention. Considering that Clary and Cara both already knew, but just hadn't really brought it up or discussed it themselves, maybe we should be asking them first?"

Emmeline agreed. "I think that's a good idea."

Celia nodded. "After you talk to them, let me know what they say."

"Whoa, whoa, whoa," Emmeline protested. "Don't you think that's something you should talk to them about?"

Celia frowned, and then her shoulders slowly sank. "I guess, considering it's my wedding and all. They'll want to know that I'm okay with it, won't they?"

"Yes, I would think so."

"Right. But that also means approaching them, and, though they are lovely girls, I must admit I find them a bit scary at times," Emmeline burst out laughing, and Celia grinned at her.

"Not really, but everybody here is so freaking talented, it makes me feel like I have absolutely nothing to offer."

"You might consider that when you're looking at everybody else, and they are probably feeling the same way about you."

"Oh, I don't think so," Celia said candidly. "The only reason I even got involved in all of this was because somehow I was chosen to carry Terkel's children."

"I think there's a lot more involved than that," Emmeline suggested, with a wry note. "But the bottom line is, we still need to have this discussion, and we're kind of running out of time."

"Yeah, we are." Celia groaned. "Crap, I may as well get to it." Then pulling out her phone, she called Clary. "Hello. I'm not sure what you're up to, but is there any chance that you and your sister could join me and Emmeline, in I guess what'll be the drawing room?"

"Sure, we'll be right there," Clary said.

Putting away her phone, Celia muttered, "I'm not sure what a drawing room is even used for anymore."

"I'm not sure either," Emmeline replied, "but we certainly don't have to continue to call it the drawing room."

"No, but, for now, it does kind of get the idea across of which room we're in," she murmured. Almost immediately the two sisters walked in, both looking calm and relaxed.

"Are you having problems?" Clary asked her. "I'm not sensing any disturbance."

"No, just a little more excitement than I was anticipating," Celia said, with a smile. "So, considering what transpired last night ..."

The two women immediately nodded.

"I'm getting married because, for whatever reason, it's become important to me to get married before the babies are born. So, what we are wondering is if you guys have considered, ... well ..." She stopped, then looked over at Emmeline. "I'm sure that you can do this much better than I could."

"I think you're doing just fine," Emmeline said, smiling at her supportively.

Celia groaned. "It just occurred to me, actually it occurred to Emmeline first, but, while we're doing all of these plans for my wedding, are you guys interested in getting married at the same time?"

THERE.

She'd done it. Celia had gotten the words out, even as the two sisters looked on in surprise. Then they slowly turned and looked at each other. "I know it's not quite what you were expecting when you came in here, but Emmeline wondered whether changes would need to be made regarding the wedding and reception, in the event anybody else wanted to tie the knot at the same time."

The two sisters didn't say a word. It was obvious that they didn't know what to say.

"And we're not trying to rush you," Emmeline said, "but, just on the off chance that this is something that you had discussed or were contemplating down the road, there is an opportunity next week."

"Is everything locked in for next week already?" Clary asked first.

"It can be pushed back a little bit," Emmeline noted, with a shrug, "if that's what you're asking. But more or less, the week after next would be the date. Pushing it later might be hard on Celia."

"It's funny," Cara said. "Neither one of us ever really planned on getting married. But I don't think we really thought we would get pregnant either and certainly not at the same time."

"I think maybe we did on some deeper level." Clary laughed. "We just didn't put any thought into when that would occur."

"Considering that it has happened already, you have raised a valid point. I'm not sure what to say." Cara fell silent.

"Neither am I," Clary agreed. "How much time do we have?" she asked Emmeline.

At that, Emmeline shrugged and replied hesitantly, "Obviously the sooner we know, the better, but within forty-eight hours for sure." She mentally nudged down the time frame that she had to work within. "If you're not inviting additional people, then it's probably not that much of a problem. It would only be trying to get paperwork ready and talking to the minister."

"You've made arrangements at the church?"

"We have," she confirmed, "but there didn't appear to be a problem with the surrounding dates, if we need to change it slightly."

The two women nodded in sync, and right now their faces looked so much alike, it was impossible to not know they were identical twins.

Celia leaned forward and cleared her throat. "One thing I do need to say is that I would be delighted to share the day with you, if that is something you want to do, but there is absolutely no pressure either way."

The women looked at her in surprise. "I was thinking that you might want that day to yourself," Clary said. "You've lost so much else."

"I've shared a lot too. As it turns out, maybe sharing is the better thing for me. In this case, I wouldn't feel like I'd lost out on a thing. So no point in going there. Obviously things didn't happen in a way I would have wanted, or thought they would, but then Terkel wasn't exactly in my orbit either. But I will not let that define my life or rob me of the joy these babies will bring."

At that, Clary nodded. "That makes perfect sense. ... We have no family either, so the numbers wouldn't change." She hesitated and looked at her sister. "I don't even know how Rick or Brody would feel."

"That's what I was just thinking." Cara nodded. "It's one thing to talk about this, but we really need to be talking to them."

"I'm not even sure that talking to Brody is what I want to do," Clary muttered.

"Meaning, you would like to be asked and not do the asking?" Emmeline asked, with a gentle smile.

"Very old-fashioned of me, isn't it?" Clary said, with a sigh.

"Not only is that quite normal and acceptable," Emmeline added, "but I would never want any of you to feel pressured into this. We can always plan another wedding down the road."

"Yes, but considering that we are both pregnant, it is something I would like to have done before the babies are born." She turned to look at her sister, and Clary nodded.

"Yes, I would prefer that myself." She shrugged, looked over at her sister. "Looks like we have some people to talk to."

"Yeah, but those aren't likely to be the easiest of conversations." Clary looked back at Emmeline and Celia. "*Forty-eight hours. We'll let you know, hopefully before that.*" Both women got up and walked out, silent.

"It went rather well actually," Emmeline said, as she surveyed Celia's face. "You did good."

"I don't know about that," Celia murmured. "Those two aren't easy to read."

"I think they've had a lot of practice on shutting down when it comes to things that they're not sure how to handle," the older woman said. "Like a lot of people."

"Right, I never did have much of a game face myself." Celia sighed. "I've always been an open book."

"Believe me. That's a nice thing. It makes life a little easier on the rest of us, since we don't have to sit here and try to guess how you're feeling."

"No, but maybe I should cultivate a little control." Celia laughed.

At that, Terkel walked into the room, then stopped. "Am I interrupting something?"

"No." Celia smiled at him. "We just spoke to the twins, asking them about joining us for the wedding. I think we should postpone the date by a few days to a week so everyone can have a chance to consider—maybe invite friends and family of their own. Plus if the wedding does get bigger, food planning, etcetera, might need to be revisited."

"Oh, good idea. I'm glad you were able to bring it up with them. How did they react?"

"I think what it'll do is stall the plans for right now," Emmeline said, as Charles joined them in the room. "I think you guys now have to pick up the baton and do something yourself."

"What do you mean?" Terkel frowned.

"Both women would like to get married, probably at the same time, or maybe together themselves in the near future, certainly before the babies come. They said as much. But the reality is, I really think they want to be asked."

"Oh, crap," Terkel said, groaning. "You know this emotional stuff is really tough on a guy, right?"

Celia beamed at him. "Yet you handle it so beautifully."

He snorted. "This is sounding like you're about to throw me under the bus."

"No," Emmeline said, turning to look at Charles. "I was thinking Charles might be the person for that."

Charles just glared at her. "Now you're trying to throw me under the bus?"

"Tit for tat," she said cheerfully.

"Did you also speak to Tasha?" Terk asked.

"No, not yet." Celia shook her head. "It seemed like a lot of pressure already."

"It is, to a certain extent." He nodded. "Kind of a confusing time for everyone."

"And I am just slowly coming out of that confusion." Celia looked up at him, with a bright smile. "And we knew about the pregnancy right from the beginning, so we've had a little bit longer to deal with it."

"Yeah, their personal relationships are relatively new," he murmured.

"Yet not necessarily," Emmeline questioned. "At least from my understanding, Tasha and Damon were an item for quite a while."

"There were undercurrents, but neither had pursued it. Now Mariana and Calum were long-term, though they'd never lived as a family until recently—after she and the little guy were kidnapped. Cal had stayed away, thinking that would keep them safe. I want to say they're married, but I can't be certain." Terk looked over at Celia, with an eyebrow raised.

"Don't look at me. I have no idea," Celia said. "Honestly, I'm still trying to get my head wrapped around who all these individual people are. I completely left out Naira and Scott when we were counting rooms the other day."

Charles smiled at her. "But you're doing magnificently."

She grinned up at him. "Charles, you are just one of those really kind people."

"I try to be." He walked over and sat down beside Emmeline. "And you are doing a lovely job as well."

She chuckled. "I don't know. It was a little touch-and-go there for a while."

"I can see that, not to mention the fact that a lot more hormones and emotions are involved than we may have realized."

"Isn't that the truth?" Emmeline said, with feeling. "When you look at it that way, it's going very well."

"Are you ever sorry that you didn't have children?" Celia asked her.

"For the longest time, yes, but I wasn't even sure I could

have children. And, for my husband, it was a definite no, so it didn't become an issue."

"You probably still could, if you wanted to."

"I'm past it now, even if I did have a partner."

"Well, it seems to me that you already do. You and Charles are a lovely couple," Celia stated. "But I get that whole *needing time* thing. Of course an opportunity just opened up." And, with that, she got up. "I find myself ravenous once again, so I'm heading to the kitchen."

Terkel, uncomfortable with the subject at hand, quickly followed.

CHARLES LOOKED OVER at Emmeline, wondering if she'd picked up on Celia's not-so-subtle hints.

Emmeline looked at him and smiled. "Sounds like our friendship is causing some talk."

"Not totally unexpected, I'm sure." He gave a slight shrug.

"I used to wonder about the future, you know? Thinking about someday, whenever I was single again, just assuming, due to the age difference, that Dean would predecease me. I always expected that you would be there waiting."

"Waiting for you? Well, I've never made any secret of that."

"No, of course not. You're far too polite for that."

"Was I supposed to then?"

"No, not at all. Sometimes things just have to happen in their own way."

"It's been enough time since Dean's passing, by anybody's measure."

"Yep, it sure has, not that I'm concerned about the opinions of others. But I am past it. Obviously I'll never forget. I spent a lot of years with him, but there comes a time to move on."

"Does that mean you're more than ready to move on, and potentially with me?" he asked hesitantly.

She leaned over, kissing him gently on the cheek. "That would be lovely."

He grinned and held her close. "And where would you like see us go to from here?" he asked curiously.

"I'm not thinking ahead. Obviously everything here will be complete chaos for a while." There was a pensive tone to her voice.

"But it won't stay that way," he reminded her. "At one point this initial confusion will ease, and they'll get into a normal pattern. Although multiple upcoming births over the next year will cause more disruption than I think they are ready for. But that doesn't have to affect us."

"No, it doesn't." They sat here, holding hands. "Having already felt like the time since he passed and the years we were together all went by so fast, if we're planning on moving forward, in whatever capacity, I don't want to be treated like a piece of porcelain that can't handle whatever is coming."

He frowned at her. "No, my dear, never that." He chuckled. "But I do believe you may be the best person to handle all the hormones and emotions going on around here."

"That may prove to be a challenge, especially as we get closer to their due dates. Although it's quite possible this marriage-before-babies thinking may be offensive to these independent modern young women, so best we keep that in mind."

He nodded. "Quite right, we may have dodged a bullet there, so to speak. However, it would be helpful if we could have a doctor brought in, particularly for the multiple births. And considering that Terkel and Celia both expect theirs to arrive early, it might even be best if you stayed here for that time period."

"Perhaps, though you do realize all these people are experienced adults with bright minds and amazing abilities of their own? The way you said that brought to mind a chaperone for a middle-school field trip."

Charles laughed out loud. "Not my intent, I assure you."

"That may be, but nonetheless I think my work here will be done fairly soon, although that will make me sad."

"In what way?" he asked. "We'll be living only minutes away."

"I guess that will be the trick, deciding how much I want to be involved after this. How much do I want to be involved here, with another stage in my life just beginning?" she asked, looking over at him, her eyes wide.

He stared at her for a moment. "And what would that stage of your life look like?" he asked.

She chuckled and leaned closer. "I'd like to spend it with you."

He reached out and held her close. "Are you sure?"

"Of course I'm sure. I knew I needed to adjust and to grieve, otherwise I wouldn't be whole," she murmured against his neck, loving the feel of being back in his arms. "It's lonely after a loss like that, but it's also something that makes you appreciate life a whole lot more."

"Oh, I agree with that. Having been through more than a few losses myself, I'm certainly not interested in waiting very long."

"You waited way too long already," she said, chuckling. "I was kind of hoping you would move faster."

"And I wanted to give you time. Dean was my friend too."

"That's right. And, in a way, that's a good thing because then, when we talk about him, we both know exactly who we're talking about, and we can honor that memory."

He smiled. "So we'll save the discussions about the future, until this mess is cleaned up here. By the way, I'll stay here for the next couple days, but I need to return home and deal with a few issues."

"Right, but thankfully it's just a few minutes away, so you can come back."

"Exactly." He chuckled. Then he got up, pulled her up into his arms, and said, "To us, down the road."

"No." She placed a finger over his lips. "To us right now. I don't know about you, but we waited long enough, and I don't want to wait anymore." He stared at her, bewildered. She chuckled and nodded. "Yes, I know exactly what I'm saying."

By then he didn't know what to say.

"But what, I need time? No, I don't. I need to grieve? I've done that. You don't want to rush me? I'm rushing you, so now I'll rush you one more time. All this talk about marriage has got me thinking."

At that, his heart started to pound. "Seriously?" he asked cautiously.

"Yes, seriously." She clasped his cheeks and pulled him ever-so-gently toward her. "I really do think it's time that we got our crap together."

"You mean, after all these years?"

"After all these years. Dean was sick for a long time, and

we knew that, but, at the same time, we also always knew that this day was coming. I know you were waiting for me." And she kissed him again and added, "Now the waiting really is over. I'm not prepared to do it any longer."

He wrapped her up and held her tightly. Soon he pulled back. "Do you want to marry with them or—" He hesitated. "Maybe we should show them how to get it done, without any fuss or problems."

"Yep." She grinned. "I happen to know that a church has an opening on Wednesday now, as we'll postpone the smaller wedding for a bigger one a week or so later."

He stared at her in surprise, and then he laughed out loud. "Do we get to invite anybody?"

"I thought we could invite everybody," she said, with a twinkle in her eyes. "Including Jonas."

"Perfect. Wednesday it is." And then he stopped and looked at her. "Tux?"

"You already have one, so absolutely."

He smiled. "What about the reception?"

"It will be here. Don't worry. I'll take care of it."

And he knew in his heart of hearts that she would. Finally it was their time.

EMMELINE WORKED STEADILY for the next few days. With Celia's wedding pushed back a week, it was a simple matter of arranging Emmeline's own wedding. The fact that she'd already had a wedding dress picked out and fitted said a lot about where the state of her mind was. She and Charles had talked about everything but marriage over the years, even as they watched her husband fall terribly ill, live for several years, then pass away, peacefully surrounded by those who loved him. And now that time was over, and she had no intention of waiting any longer.

That was one of the lessons learned from watching somebody pass on, while you were right there with them every step of the way. Emmeline had been reminded of just how precious life was and how quickly she could lose it all. Quite unexpectedly in some cases.

She had enjoyed a great life with Dean. But there'd always been that sense that she had married into his life instead of having a life alongside him. She had adapted at every step of the way because it was expected. That's just the way things were done, but yet this time was different. And she couldn't wait. Charles was a special person, and she knew that their life would always be full of intrigue because he would not stop doing what he did. And neither would she try to get him to change. She figured that she might stay on with Terkel, maybe as a consultant for handling all the renovations and whatnot going on. Then, down the road, that would be something they could take another look at.

The timing for her wedding was perfect, as far as she was concerned, and she couldn't wait. The other women had been so excited when they found out what she was doing and what her plans were that everybody had pitched in to try and make it as special as possible.

When Wednesday dawned, bright and sunny, it was almost like a sign from above.

She looked up, smiled, and whispered, "Thank you, dear." With her ride to the church and everything in place, the ceremony went off without a hitch. She chuckled, as the other women were more excited in some ways than she had really expected, but, as Charles always said, *Everybody loves a wedding.*

CHAPTER 9

TERKEL STOOD OUTSIDE the church after the ceremony, smiling as Charles walked over to him with a satisfied grin. "Bet that was a long time coming," Terk stated.

"Too long." Charles nodded. "However, no way I would rock the boat while Dean was dying."

"No, sometimes things have to happen the way they must happen," Terk murmured. "You two have a lot of good years left."

"I hope so. That's the way it's done, if you're ready to jump on board."

"Next week," Terkel agreed. "I'm glad we adjusted the time frame, giving you two an opportunity to get married first. Besides a few extra days for us isn't a problem."

"Emmeline wouldn't have done it if it would cause problems. And, of course, I've been worried about something going wrong to stop everything in its tracks. But no sign of the one man?"

Terk shook his head. "No, and we've been looking. Security has been a nightmare, what with the number of workmen in and out of the place, but everyone has memorized that other guy's face, so if he does show up ..."

"Good." Charles nodded.

At that, Celia walked toward them, with a gentle smile. "Wasn't so scary, was it?" she murmured to Terkel.

He chuckled, put an arm on her shoulders, and pulled her close. "Nope, I can't wait." And he kissed her gently.

Charles added, "It seems like the other women are more than excited to have had the first wedding go off without a hitch, so I suspect there may be a lot more to come."

"We'll see, although I'm not sure what we'll do without you two for the next few days," Celia said, as she hugged Emmeline. "It was a lovely ceremony. I'm so happy for both of you."

Emmeline nodded. "Which is why I told you that we could postpone going away until after your wedding."

"No, not required. You guys go have a nice weekend, and we'll see you on Monday."

"That's the plan," Charles stated, with a huge smile.

A few minutes later, Terkel and Celia stood together and watched as the two of them headed off. "They pulled off a wedding really fast, didn't they?" he murmured.

She nodded.

"And easy and smooth. They chose not to have a reception though. Was that because of us?" he asked curiously.

"I don't think so," she replied. "They've both been waiting for a very long time. I think they wanted to maximize their time together, especially since they will be back on Monday. ... It had to be tough for both Charles and Emmeline, knowing that, in order to marry the person of your dreams and to move on in life, your mutual best friend, the person who you loved and spent a lifetime with, had to pass on." She frowned. "And it makes me wonder about that marriage, their relationship, about how that worked out for Dean. I understand he was very ill for the final years of his life. I mean, knowing his two friends would probably marry, was that imminent second marriage for Emmeline something that made the later part of Dean's life even more difficult for him?"

"I don't think so," Terk said. "I never asked Charles about it, but he did volunteer that Dean knew perfectly well what would happen when he was gone, and he had already given them his blessings. Apparently the three of them had been best friends for ages, so it made Dean feel better to know that Emmeline wouldn't be alone. Plus, Dean was fourteen years her senior, so he had to accept the probability that she would outlive him and would marry again. Although marrying Dean's best friend might have been a sore spot, even if just for a moment."

"I kind of like that, how Dean gave them his blessing," she murmured. "And good for her for finding true love that will stand the test of time."

"It really will, won't it?" he asked, looking at her.

She nodded. "Even I got the premonition on that one."

He chuckled. "Sometimes I don't get them, even when I think I will. It's frustrating, as visions can be clear as a bell, then suddenly just darkness for a long time."

"That's part of the mystery of what we do," she murmured. "You can always count on confusing messages all the time."

"Except for one," he said, pulling her into his arms. "Us."

"One more week, then it's our turn."

"Did you hear from anybody else wanting to get married next week?"

"Things kind of got blown up when Emmeline announced that they were getting married, as she felt really bad that she was preempting me." He looked at her in surprise. She shrugged. "I know, right? It didn't matter to me in the least. I was so happy to have them get married so that it made it easier on me."

"How do you figure that?" he asked curiously.

"I was really happy to know that they would follow through on what they needed to do themselves. And they didn't want any fuss or mess about it all, as they'd planned this for a long time, but hadn't really reached the point of doing anything about it."

"Of course not. Charles was waiting for her. She was waiting for Charles." Terk burst out laughing. "Right? So what does that say about the rest of our group?"

"I don't know. I think this will spur a whole lot of change though."

"Good change or bad?" he muttered.

"Is there such a thing as bad change?"

"In a way, maybe not. I hadn't realized how much I was struggling against change right before my world blew up."

"And now you're fine with it?" she asked curiously.

"Adapting. Like the idea of a private company seemed unattainable, but here we are. Having a family was something I never seriously considered, and now look. I don't know that I ever would have pursued either without the catastrophic events that put us here."

Soon the rest of the extended team gathered around. They all decided it was time to head back home, and everyone was moving toward their vehicles, including Jonas, who had shown up for the wedding on the spur of the moment.

He approached Terk, a smirk on his face. "Got an early wedding gift for you."

"Is that right?" Terk asked, one eyebrow raised.

"Followed the money trail provided by our chatty prisoner Bill and caught Roger, the guy paying for that remaining hit on you and your team."

"Appreciate it."

"That should tie things up for you."

Terk huffed. "Could be more such hits out there. After bad seeds in my own government tried to blow up my team and me, that will always leave a bad taste in my mouth. And always make us extra vigilant." He didn't mention how more cloned babies could be out there, using Terk's harvested sperm and maybe even harvested eggs from Celia. Terk shook his head.

Jonas grimaced. "Understood. Keep your ear to the ground. I'll be listening too." And, with a nod, he left.

Damon and Tasha walked over toward Terk and Celia. "Can we have a moment?"

Tasha asked, "So, remember that question you asked earlier?"

"Yes, I do," Celia answered. "Have you come up with an answer?" But she already knew.

"It's a yes," Tasha beamed. "That is, if we can still get it done at the same time. I was hoping that, since things just got pushed back a little bit, maybe it was still possible."

"I don't think it was a pushback as much as everybody assumed that at least some of you might want to join in, and a few extra days might make things a little easier."

"And you're okay with that? You really won't have a problem with sharing your day?"

"Absolutely no problem," Celia said, with a bright smile. "This whole journey has been about sharing. But how about you?"

"I'm absolutely okay with it." Tasha smiled. "And, like you, I just want to get it done."

"So, you've had some time to adjust now to your pregnancy?"

"No, hell no." She patted her still-flat tummy. "And I'm still not sure you guys are correct with that diagnosis, but I haven't done anything about finding out for sure because … I guess I really want you to be correct."

"We're correct." Celia nodded. "Yet it's easy enough to pick up a home pregnancy test somewhere."

"No, I don't need to do that, and I'm happy to just wait and let nature take its course. And, besides, I've worked with Terk for a long time and have seen him be right about an awful lot of things."

"Let's hope nature doesn't take too long, *huh?*" Celia added.

"Right," Tasha agreed. "I hadn't really put any thought into having a child, and it certainly wouldn't have been something I'd planned, but the longer I have to get used to the idea, the more I'm over the moon."

"Perfect," Celia murmured. "Then I suggest we contact Emmeline via text and let her know that it's a go, although I'm pretty sure she is probably already planning for it."

At that, Terkel nodded. "Charles did tell me that they were planning for multiple brides, so they wanted to get in a quick honeymoon break, before it came down to the craziness of next week."

"Do you think they have abilities too?" Damon asked curiously.

"Not so much abilities in the way that we think of them." Terkel smiled. "However, what they have is the experience and wisdom that comes with age."

"Right." Damon grinned. "Something that we have yet to tap."

At that, Terk burst out laughing. "Isn't that the truth. We're heading back to the house. How about you guys?"

"Absolutely." Tasha started toward the vehicles and then shook her head. "I'm so much more tired now."

"Exactly." Celia gave her a knowing look, as she waddled at a much slower pace. "Enjoy getting some extra rest while you can. Once these babies come, I'm not sure we'll get any sleep for a while."

"Probably not," Tasha replied, "but how exciting to have babies together." And, with that, they climbed into their vehicles and headed out on the short drive home.

As Terkel pulled into the castle, Celia looked over at him. "I see a lot of people getting married at the same time."

He stopped, considering her. "You think the twin sisters will get married too, at the same time?"

"I don't think so," she said solemnly, "but they're keeping it a fairly guarded secret at the moment."

"I suspect they have the ability to do that in ways we don't even begin to know about."

"They do have abilities that I've never seen before. We can learn an awful lot from them."

He smiled at her. "Glad to see you still thinking in terms of learning and growing and changing."

"Absolutely," Celia said. "We have to. I think our biggest challenges will be the fact that our kids also have abilities."

He looked at her in surprise. "You know that already?"

"I know that already, don't you?"

He thought about it for a moment and then nodded. "Oh, yeah, we'll have fun."

"Especially when there will be others born with abilities too."

He started to chuckle. "That will be chaos."

"But fun chaos," she argued. Still laughing, they headed inside the castle.

THE NEXT MORNING, when Celia was sitting down, nursing a cup of tea in the kitchen, Mariana approached. "Hey," Celia said, as she watched Little Calum climb up to the table beside her. "How are you two doing?" she asked Mariana.

"We're good. Wasn't that a lovely and simple affair yesterday?"

"Yes, and that's what we're planning for ourselves, as well."

"Celia, did you consider that maybe other people might want to get married? How do you feel about sharing your day?"

Celia grinned. "The more, the merrier, as far as I'm concerned." She studied Mariana's face. "Have you spoken to Damon and Tasha?"

"No, why?"

"Oh, they've decided to get married at the same time as Terk and I do. But, if you hadn't heard about that, what are you really asking about?"

Mariana laughed. "Calum and I were talking about it. Technically we are still legally married, but, now that we're together again, we would like to renew our vows."

"Oh, I love that," Celia cried out, smiling brightly, as she stared at one of her new friends. "It will be an absolute blessing to have it at the same time. And, of course, the reception is back here afterward, if that works for you. And you don't have to prepare a thing for it. Emmeline is having it catered."

"That all sounds lovely and really fun. I'm all for it."

"Perfect. You fill Calum in, and I'll text Emmeline." Then she stopped and looked over at Mariana. "Unless you wanted to. The question Emmeline will have involves the guest list. Is there anyone you want to invite who isn't already coming?"

Immediately Mariana shook her head. "Sadly, no," she said. "No family for either of us."

"That makes it easy then." Celia tapped out a text message to Emmeline.

"Thank you." At that, Mariana headed out but stopped at the door. "I just wondered ..."

"Wondered what?" Celia asked, looking up from her phone.

"I just wondered if you saw if I was pregnant—or soon to be?"

Mariana really wants a second child. "You mean, if you are pregnant *now?*" Celia asked Mariana. At her nod, Celia tilted her head to the side and then shrugged. "Honestly, not that it means anything, but I'm not getting anything right now." She watched Mariana's face fall. "It could be really early," she immediately explained. "Sometimes we catch it early, and sometimes it's weeks later."

"Right." Mariana forced a smile. "Maybe I'll be one of the lucky ones down the road." And, with that, she disappeared.

That conversation was something that Celia wondered about as the day went on. When she had a chance to talk to Terk later on, she explained what had happened.

"Oh, now that's interesting, and really why wouldn't they want to get their vows renewed." He nodded. "That makes perfect sense and sounds like a great idea."

At dinner that night, which was a simple affair, Celia announced to everyone that Tasha and Damon were joining her and Terk in getting married, plus, at the same time, Mariana and Calum were renewing their vows.

"Wow." There were surprised looks, and everybody shrugged.

"We really have no other family for us other than this team," Mariana said, "and life's been pretty tough these last few years, especially these last couple months. Now we're all making this new beginning, so it just seemed like the right thing for us to do."

As Calum reached out a hand and closed his fingers around hers, at the same time he took an extra fork away from Little Calum. "At some point in time, this little guy will need a sibling."

"The sooner, the better, as far as I'm concerned," Mariana replied. "Having them too far apart is like starting all over again."

At that, Terkel looked at her and Calum and around the room and frowned. When he didn't say anything, Celia wondered about it.

Then Cara spoke up. "We've made a decision too," she announced, and they all looked at Cara and Clary with interest.

Clary smiled. "Celia, if you are sure you don't mind sharing your day even more, both my sister and I would like to get married too. And, yes, our future husbands have agreed," she said, smiling at the men in question.

At that came more cheers, as hope and joy spread around the big table.

Terkel looked over at Celia and smiled. "You're pretty

smart. You know that, right?"

"Oh, I don't know about that. Charles and Emmeline brought it up."

"Wow, and I can see why," Terk noted, "because this is huge. Now there are five of us."

"No," Wade said. "It's six now." And there was laughter all around, as yet another voice piped up.

"Make that seven," Lorelei called out.

And that left only one couple. As everybody turned and stared at them, Naira held up her hands. "Hey, I was leaving it up to him to decide."

"Me?" Scott stared at her in astonishment. "I thought you didn't want to."

"Of course I do." She laughed. "I just didn't want you to feel pressured into it."

"Well, in that case," he said, "let's make it a full sweep."

Naira jumped up and landed in his lap.

"That's good because," Terkel stated, as everybody looked at him, "one, we'll need a name for our business and for the compound. Also, with so many babies coming so fast, we'll need more help, and we need to work on adjusting the layout here accordingly."

"We do, indeed," Celia said, nodding, "There is lots to do."

At that, Terkel stood up, turned to look around the room, then froze. "Holy crap." He looked at Clary and Cara. "Do you guys see what I'm seeing?"

At that, Celia stood up, walked around to his side and slipped her arm through his, then started to laugh. "I don't know what we started, but we'll have to find a way to put the brakes on it too."

"What are you talking about?" The twins got up and

stood on either side of them and surveyed the rest of the room. Then one after the other, they started to laugh.

"Oh my God," Clary cried out, staring at the roomful of confused faces, and then back again at Terk. "Did you know this would happen?"

"No," he said, fascinated. "Believe me. I had no clue. But now that it's happening, Celia is right. We have to make sure that it doesn't continue beyond what everybody wants."

"That'll be an interesting challenge," Celia murmured.

As everybody stared at the group, Gage spoke up in a testy voice. "I don't know what you're talking about," he snapped, "and you're making me very nervous. So can you just spill it?"

"Well," Terk started, and then he fell silent. He looked at the others and said, "I don't know how you all feel about telling everybody."

"I think at this point we have to," Celia said. Then she looked over at Mariana. "So remember when I told you no earlier because I wasn't sure. I can tell you right now that it's a definite yes."

Mariana looked at her in shock and then jumped up to her feet in joy. "Seriously?"

Celia nodded. "Yes, seriously. As always, when we get together, the combined energy is easier to identify." She smiled. "So in your case, it's a yes."

Mariana looked over at Calum with a bright smile.

"What was that all about?" Calum asked suspiciously.

"I'm pregnant," she cried out. She danced around the room, screaming, "I'm pregnant. I'm pregnant. I'm pregnant."

Calum stared at her in shock, then bounced out of his chair, grabbed her, and spun her around. Then they both looked at the rest of the group. Cal turned toward Terkel. "How many of us are pregnant?" he asked hesitantly.

Terk looked at him. "That's what I mean. It's one thing to be pregnant and delighted about it right now," he murmured, "but this isn't something that we thought would happen ever."

At that, the rest of the people in the room continued to stare at him, and he nodded.

"I don't know how to tell you guys, but, from what I can see, every freaking one of us is about to have babies."

CHAPTER 10

T HAT NIGHT CELIA curled up against Terk. "I think they are all happy."

He snorted, as he tucked her up closer. "I hope so. They seemed to be, but it's a huge initial shock for all of them. You and I have had weeks, months to adapt. For some of them, that is ahead of them. But now Marianna? She's thrilled."

"She had asked me earlier today, and I couldn't see it clearly. I was getting more of a question mark answer, so I couldn't give her the response she was really hoping for. But for the others? ... Wow. And somehow we have to shut down this baby-making factory after this."

"Yeah, you got any idea on how to do that?"

"I think it'll require the twins' help. As in finding some way to guard against such a thing."

He stilled under her hand. She shifted so she could look up at him. "What?"

"*Guardians*," he murmured, then relaxed. "That fits." Just then he sat up, and she grunted at the sudden movement. But Terk was in warrior mode—and buck naked. He raced to the door.

She called out, "Here."

He glanced back, as she tossed his boxers at him. He dragged them on, as he stepped out of the room.

In her head, he said, *Lock up. We have an intruder.*

She bolted to her feet and locked the bedroom door. That would explain the weird fuzziness going on in her head. Like a drumbeat she wanted to ignore but couldn't. With so much craziness all evening, it's no wonder the negative energy had slipped by them.

Still it was concerning. Unable to return to bed, she pulled on her robe and stepped to the window and opened her senses.

Bitch.

She stepped back, hearing that voice strong in her mind.

Whoever was out there was pissed, letting his anger override common sense. He was back for round two. Instantly she knew who the intruder was. *It's the man MI6 released,* she told Terk.

Yes, I see the energy signature. He's in the kitchen where he found you all last time.

Do you want me to come down?

No. We've got this.

Who is with you?

Calum, Wade, and Gage.

Ah, so he can deal with the men this time. Fun. And Celia was almost sorry she wasn't there. The intruder had been shocked and confused by how the women had acted and how they had treated him. He wouldn't like the reception the men would give him any better.

With a fat smile she hung up her robe and sat against the headboard and waited.

Terk wouldn't be long.

TERK, HIS MEN at his side, approached the kitchen and stepped inside. The intruder was in the pantry muttering to himself, "Gotta find a place to hide. A place those bitches, … no, make that *witches*, can't find me."

There was a general banging and clanging, as if he were trying to move pots to make a space for himself.

Gage snorted softly under his breath. "We should contact Jonas."

"We'll fix this first so this guy never comes back, then call Jonas." Deliberately Terk coughed loud.

The silence from the pantry was deafening. Then a head poked out from inside. His glare turned to fear instantly.

"Hungry?" Terk asked calmly, as he crossed his arms across his bare chest.

The intruder stepped out, his gun up and pointing at them. "Where are they?"

"Where are who?" Calum asked in a super helpful voice.

"The women. Those damn witches."

"Witches or bitches?" This time Wade spoke but his voice was much less than friendly.

"Both," the gunman snapped, waving his gun around. "They laughed at me."

As if that made total sense for his return, Terk nodded. "Yeah, that can be infuriating."

The gunman nodded, his gun pointed at Terk. "Right? They need to be put in their place," he snapped. "They need to respect the gun. They didn't. Not at all."

"Yeah, I can see how that might be a problem for you," Terk noted.

And it slowly dawned on the gunman that none of the men appeared bothered by the gun either. Or his presence. He frowned at them, looked at the weapon in his hand, then back at the four men. "Why are you guys not scared of it? It's real. It's not a toy." He brandished it in the air in a threatening movement, only to lower it when he saw the smiles on the men's faces.

"Nope. I'm sure it's not a toy," Terk murmured in a gentle tone, "but you really don't want to go in this direction."

"Yeah?" he snapped belligerently. "And why not?"

"Because, like the women, we don't care about that piddly gun," Calum said softly. "Nor do we like intruders in our house."

"The windows shouldn't be boarded up then. And one of them wasn't very strong at all."

"Right, the new windows were delayed. So that's how you got in?" Terk nodded. "And, of course, in all the chaos, the energy has been firing double-time but not clear enough in the chaos to see you approaching."

"Energy? See me approaching?" Now he looked a little worried. "You're not like them, are you?"

"Like who?" Wade asked helpfully.

"Those witches." But as the gunmen studied the four men before him, his shoulders sagged. Then his eyes widened, as he studied the air where the men used to be. "Oh my God, where did you go?"

Terk laughed, as Calum and Wade threw up a simple smoke screen. "Oh, we are here—or are we?" Terk asked, throwing his voice from inside the pantry.

The gunman shrieked and pivoted, reacting wildly and started firing blindly into the small storage room.

Until he realized the gun—although the trigger was pulling back with each movement—had nothing coming out. He swiveled almost in slow motion to see the four men once again, standing clearly before him.

And sirens outside came down the long driveway.

He looked at the men, at the gun, at the men again, and asked in a low, pitiful voice, "Am I crazy?"

"You were crazy to ever come here," Wade snapped. "And even crazier to come a second time."

The intruder slowly placed the gun on the kitchen table and raised his hands. "I need to leave." His tone was almost formal. "Sorry to have disturbed you." And he bolted for the doorway.

And ended up flat on the floor, as both feet went out from under him.

"So sorry," Terk said in a cheerful voice, as Wade left to answer the front door. "Or maybe not. But the cops want to see you. I doubt you'll get free a second time quite so easily." Terk turned to see several police officers coming into the kitchen.

As soon as the intruder saw them, he jumped to his feet and started babbling, "Witches live here. They are warlocks." He dramatically pointed at the four men. "They stopped my gun from firing, and they went *poof* and disappeared ..." His arms flailed about as he tried to explain what his words couldn't.

One of the cops whispered under his breath, "Oh, blimey."

"His gun is on the table, complete with his fingerprints. And I think our unwanted guest needs some special professional help," Terk suggested in a light tone. "Do see that he gets what he needs, please, officers."

And, with that, the cops snagged the gunman's arms and dragged him out of the house, while he kept screaming about magic and evil ...

"What do you think?" Calum asked. "Is that the end of it with him?"

Terk tilted his head to the side, waiting for an answer, then nodded. "Yep, it sure is. He'll spend months to years in and out of mental hospitals, trying to reconcile what he saw."

"Good. Sounds like just the place for him." Wade walked toward the stairs. "I don't know about you guys, but we've got a hell of a lot of work to be done before the weddings. I, for one, need sleep." And he headed back to his bedroom.

Following behind Calum, Wade, and Gage all split off to their rooms with a *Good night*, and Terk carried on to his.

As he walked into the bedroom, he found Celia, curled up in bed, sound asleep.

As he crawled in beside her, he realized explanations could wait until tomorrow. Then a gentle energy whisper slipped through his head. *No need. Sleep. All is well.*

And, with that, he tucked her up against him and slept.

CHAPTER 11

C ELIA WOKE ON her wedding day, her heart full and a smile on her face. She rolled over, looked at Terkel. "Ready for this?"

"Never." He grinned at her. "Yet, at the same time, I can't wait."

"Oh, I get it." She reached a hand out for his and placed it over her belly.

"Somebody else is ready to go too." He chuckled, gently rubbing her smooth skin. He hopped up and then stopped, looked at her. "You just rest. I'll go get your coffee."

"I'll be fine. I'll just get up and have a shower and start getting ready."

"We have a lot of company."

"We sure do," she said, "but, once Ice arrived, she took charge, along with Emmeline, and it's been great," she murmured. "You have the best friends."

He nodded. "I sure do. It helps that Merk's wife, Katina, came over."

"Are you kidding?" Celia laughed. "Between Bullard's clan, and the man himself, plus Ice's unexpected arrival, even though we've got extra people, they're all doing so much to make things happen that it's been a huge help."

"They're good people," he murmured.

"Did you ever hear how Katina feels about her pregnancy? About it being twins?"

"Nope, I sure haven't. I expected that they would just deal with it, like the rest of us." He tugged his shirt over his head.

"Yeah, we'll have to find another way to deal with all that too." She frowned and shook her head.

He grinned. "And figure out how to stop it."

"Yeah, not that children aren't blessings and that we might want more later, but this teamwide energy-enhanced reproductive cycle is a bit worrying and needs some barriers, hopefully before we're completely overrun with kids." She shifted on the bed. She stopped, then looked at him. "You're okay with twins, right?"

"Of course. How could I not be okay with the twins? I am a twin after all." Terk nodded. "I really don't think that's even a question right now."

"I just … There's always that bit of doubt because of the way it all happened."

"I love that our sons will soon be here." He quickly finished dressing, then leaned over and gave her gentle kisses. "Now get some rest." With that, he was gone.

She smiled because, of course, he had completely ignored her statement about getting up, having a shower, and getting dressed, but then he was a little busy with a million other things to do too. Because, even though the wedding was happening, they hadn't been able to stop work from proceeding on the rehab of the castle, plus ongoing security issues and all that it entailed, particularly when they had so much skilled help on hand. Everybody needed to pitch in and help get some things done faster.

So, that's what was going on. Even Charles and Emmeline were here. In fact, everybody was. Celia laughed as she got up, had a shower, put her hair up in a big bun that she would deal with later, then headed down to the kitchen. As soon as she got there, she was engulfed in hugs.

Ice gave her a critical once-over. "You're looking pretty good," she said, with a big grin.

"You mean blooming?" Celia chuckled.

"Absolutely blooming."

"It's so good to see you, and I can't believe you came all this way."

"What, and miss your wedding day?" Ice scolded.

"I just knew that, with traveling being what it is, it might not be practical."

"Ah, nothing to it." She grinned. "Although we brought the kids, hoping that, with Little Calum here, it would be okay."

Celia held back her hysterical laughter. "Children are always welcome here. I'm pretty sure Little Calum is delighted to have somebody his age to play with." At that, she turned to find Little Calum and one of Ice's sons, both sitting up on the two chairs at the counter, stirring bowls of something. "I'm not even sure I want to ask what it is."

"You're probably better off not to." Ice studied the boys, with a proud smile.

"Now we have a lot of brides to get ready—and grooms as well. We have rides ready for the weddings, and we've got food happening everywhere," Ice murmured. "There are so many people to feed, and honestly, once you guys get fully operational, hosting weddings on site could be a regular occasion, a side gig for you." Ice laughed at her own joke.

"Wow," Celia murmured. Everywhere she looked, there were people. Some she knew. Some she didn't, but everybody she knew had come for the wedding and to be a part of setting up their new home. "It's gorgeous," Celia added, as she looked around, seeing everybody and all the smiles. "You're blessed to have so many friends."

"We are blessed to have both friends and family. But, since you have joined the family, no matter how it came about"—Ice smiled—"enjoy. You're a part of us too."

And that's when Celia realized it was true. There had never been family for her, but she'd come all this way, and now look at this. She had a ton of family now, and they were all here to make her day perfect. She got misty-eyed, as she thought about it.

Ice just chuckled as she looked on. "Go on now. Time to get changed. I know that, when those tears start, you won't stop."

And, with that, Celia was shooed away.

Back up in her room, she dressed and took time and rested as much as she thought she could. But when someone knocked on the door, and she answered, she found Emmeline.

"We have two stylists here, for hair and makeup." And, with that, she gently guided Celia into a chair in another room that had been set up as a beauty center, with soft calming music playing from somewhere. Celia was joined with the other brides-to-be and nonalcoholic champagne was shared by all. And even though it would be a small wedding, apparently it would come with all the bells and whistles. By the time she could even turn around, she realized it was time to go to the church. Hours had gone by, but they were exciting, fun-filled hours that she had never thought to ever experience in her life.

By the time the motorcade headed toward the church, Celia's long limo full of brides, they all looked at each other with almost a sense of acceptance and joy.

"We're doing this!"

Celia looked at them all. "If I didn't have a chance to say it before, I do want to say it now." Celia beamed. "Thank you all for coming and for making my day easier."

"Are you kidding?" Mariana beamed at her. "Thank you all for this because I never would have gotten Calum back to the altar." The rest burst out laughing.

"I think it's also important to realize," Sophia said gently, "that we're all here because we want to be here, and we're all here because we're sisters in one form or another."

At that came more tears in the back of Celia's throat. "That is the nicest thing anybody has ever said to me."

Sophia reached for her and gave her a gentle hug. "Hey, we've got years ahead of us now. And I fully intend to enjoy every one of them."

And, with that, they arrived at the church. Then slowly, with all of them carefully disembarking and setting their dresses to right, they heard the music starting inside. They looked at each other as one, and Charles stood proudly with them. "Are we ready?"

"Hell no." Celia laughed. "But I'm game."

And, with that, they all laughed and followed the wedding march into the church.

Celia beamed. This was the first day of the rest of her life, and it had never looked better.

EPILOGUE

I T HAD BEEN weeks since the chaotic eight-couple wedding and the biggest party that Terkel had ever attended in his life. That it was for him and his friends and his team had filled his heart with joy and had reminded him what was important in life. Now, sitting in the servants' kitchen—still awaiting the final tweaks on the reno of the big main kitchen—having coffee with Gage, Terk got a mental picture of his hugely pregnant wife, and he realized that they had a ton more to do. He looked over at Gage. "We need to do a current assessment of what still needs to happen here in the next little bit."

"We're also getting calls for help," Gage replied.

"What do you mean?" Terk asked him.

Gage frowned. "He's called twice today already."

"Who?"

"Jonas. He wants to talk to you."

"What does he want?"

"I don't know. I've been pushing him off because, as soon as I call him back, it'll be a case of our time here coming to an end."

"It'll change for sure sometime soon," Terk murmured. "We can't get out of that."

"I know. I know." Gage grinned. "I was trying to postpone it though."

Terk burst into laughter, nodding his head. "It's been pretty special, I know. Crazy, at times, with all this work on the place and all. It sounds like even those who left for proper honeymoons after the wedding are back today."

"I know, and that return will change things too," Gage murmured.

Even as they talked, Damon and Tasha walked into the small kitchen, all smiles and hugs. "You should try getting away every once in a while, Terk," Damon suggested.

"And I would," Terk agreed, "but, right now, this place is still a nightmare."

"I don't know." Damon looked around. "It's looking phenomenal."

"We're getting there. Not quite there yet, but we're close." On that note, the rest of the team filed in, all grabbing coffee and joining in on the conversation. Terk smiled, looking at Damon and Tasha, and asked, "Are you guys ready to get back to work?"

They both nodded. "Yeah, it was good to get away, but honestly we missed you guys," Tasha said, as she walked over and gave Terk a big hug. "And now, after confirming that I'm pregnant, I'm so excited. I really just want to be home with family."

Damon nodded. "Even when I told her that we could stay longer, she was like, *Nope, I want to go home.* So that's where we're at, and that's good—because you really do want to know who your friends are and where they'll be in these times."

"Exactly, and, with that, I'm heading upstairs. I might even have a nap." Tasha laughed, rolling her eyes, and quickly disappeared.

"She hasn't quite adjusted to the fact that she has zero

energy. And it's still early in the pregnancy," Damon said, watching her leave. "So she's not sure what that means."

"It means she's pregnant." Celia chuckled, as she waddled in to join them.

Damon took one look at Celia and winced. "My God, I sure hope Tasha's not carrying twins."

"I have no clue what she's carrying." Celia smirked. "And, right now, it's all I can do to keep my own world somewhat contained."

He laughed and nodded. "I hear you there. So what's going on?" Damon asked Terk.

"What's going on is that Jonas is being insistent this morning. He's called a couple times already." Just then Terkel looked at his phone. "I had mine off," he confessed. Reluctantly he turned it back on, and it rang immediately. "Well, here we go." He frowned, switching his cell to Speaker. "Jonas, what's up?"

"What you can do for us is give us some help," he snapped in a crisp tone. "We have two escaped prisoners."

"More escaped prisoners?" Terk asked, his tone drawled.

"Hey, they were being transported from France," he said, "and now the shit's hit the fan."

"Who are these prisoners?"

"They're wanted by Interpol, but we wanted first crack to prosecute them, so they were being transported here. Yet somehow they escaped."

"Did they go via the channel or the ferry?"

"Yeah, we're still trying to get the details on all that. I'm sending over the information I have right now." He added, "We really need these guys, and we need them back *now*."

"And why are you calling us?" Terk asked.

At that, Jonas's voice slowed down, and, with a sigh, he

said, "Because there's a problem."

"What kind of problem?"

"We weren't supposed to have them in the first place," he admitted reluctantly. "So none of this can come back to us."

"Great, so we're supposed to do a catch-and-retrieve mission for MI6, and you don't want anybody, like the DGSE, to know it's for you guys?"

"Not only can the French *not* know that these guys were coming to us but they can't know that you were hired by us. So I hope you guys have your banking set up because we have the funds set up and ready to pay you."

When Jonas named a figure, everybody in the room was stunned, and they just stared at each other, eyebrows sky-high.

"Fifty percent now, the other half when you bring them in. I can't tell you how important it is for your future of working with us if you can do this," he stated. "And, if you can't, then I can't guarantee too much more work."

"Send us what you've got," Terkel responded, "and I'll see who I've got available."

"If you don't have anybody available because you're all still sitting in whatever marital bliss thing you guys have got going on over there, not to mention the baby factory," he added on a laugh, "you need to hire somebody."

"Oh, I definitely need to hire somebody," Terk agreed, "but still I wouldn't send them out on a mission all alone. We have to make sure they're good enough to even go on a job in our name."

"That's your problem," Jonas replied. "You have literally four hours to get back to me with your acceptance of this job—well, no, you *had* four, but now you only have one. You would have had longer, but you didn't answer your damn phone." And, with that, he hung up.

Terk looked around at the rest of the group. "You heard the figures."

"Yeah, we sure did," Gage said, "and we definitely need satellite money, so I'm willing." He looked around at the others. "Who's coming with me?"

"Do you think this is a two-man job or four?" Wade asked.

"Even if it is four, we don't want to leave this place unprotected. An awful lot of very important people are here," Terk said, with a smile.

"Right," the expanded team all said in unison.

"I was contacted by someone named Riff not too long ago, looking to be part of our team." Terk looked down at his cell. "It's one of the reasons I had turned this off, so I could think about it. I just wasn't sure that we were ready to hire anybody. However, if we are, Levi and Bullard have a recommendation for us too. His name is Radar. Apparently he's done jobs for both men but isn't a great permanent fit for either. Three guesses as to why?"

Celia laughed. "Like we need three. Still, are we ready to go this route?"

"Probably not, but, if we take on a bunch of rush jobs, like this one from Jonas," Damon added, "then we need more people. Particularly given the pregnancies right now and working the kinks out of the castle security system."

"I know," Terk agreed. "I just didn't want to get started down that interview and vetting road already."

"I don't think we have a choice," Damon said. "What's the deal with this other guy, Riff?"

Hearing that guy's name, Wade stepped forward. "I know him. I spent time in Iraq with him." Then he stopped and frowned. "He was always a little different."

"He's definitely a little different," Terkel confirmed, "because his abilities are a little different."

"He has abilities?" Damon looked at his boss and friend in delight. "So how come you haven't hired him before?"

"A couple reasons. Before, he would have had to pass muster with the CIA, and that would never happen."

"Why is that?" Damon asked.

"Because he was and still is the main suspect in a murder case, and they steer clear of anything like that."

"Whose murder?" Gage asked.

"His fiancée," Terk replied calmly.

"And did he kill her?"

"No, he didn't," he replied, "but it affected him badly."

"Yeah, you're not kidding," Gage added. "Can you imagine? Not only dealing with the grief and the loss but you also now have to deal with the fact that the rest of the world suspects you."

"Exactly. I know he didn't do it, and he knows he didn't do it. But it's really a matter of whether any of you will have an issue with it."

"If you trust him, I'm willing to give him a try," Damon said. "Send Riff out with me. I'll put him through the wringer. Hell, if I'm going alone, give me both of them. Radar sounds interesting. Do we know anything else about him? Not that it matters if both Bullard and Levi recommended him. This would be a great test run."

"Yeah, but we can't have this job messed up—not when it's the first for Jonas and MI6." Damon looked around the table. "Votes."

"Yes," Celia said. "We need good men, and, with these references, we're not likely to get any better."

The others nodded.

"There's one more thing," Terkel said. "And it's one of

the reasons Riff called me in the first place. He'll be looking for help as well."

"What kind of help?"

"He still hasn't found out who killed his fiancée. As you can imagine, that is an issue he needs to resolve before he can move on."

"If he comes to work for us, it goes without saying that we'd give him a hand too." Wade looked around at the rest of the group. "I say, give him a call, and let's get started. Time is short, and this gives us a hell of a jumping-off point, and one we need."

"Any objections?" Terk asked, looking around at the others.

All shook their heads in silence.

"Okay then." Terk studied each face around him, but he found only support. "I'll give Riff and Radar a call, and one of you call Jonas, please. Tell him, if he's got that kind of money sitting there, we'll have no problem taking it off their hands." Then, with a big fat grin, he added, "Looks like we're in business."

"We still need a company name though," Wade said. "We have legal paperwork to set up."

"And I have a name." Terk hesitated. "It's partly from this castle. Above the door in Latin it says, *In times of war, ... we guard.*"

The others looked at him in surprise.

"I was thinking *Guardian Security.*"

"And for short"—Wade gave the rest of the team a fat grin—"the Guardians."

This concludes Book 9 of Terkel's Team: Terkel's Triumph.

Read a sneak peek from Radar: Terkel's Guardian, Book 1

Radar: Terkel's Guardian (Book 1)

RADAR, OR ROBERT Dagliesh, a name he barely recognized anymore, studied the lanes of traffic speeding past him. He was on the Calais side of the tunnel, crossing from France to England, and in the immediate vicinity of where the four people had disappeared. He'd walked as close as he could get to where the vehicle had been found, then towed to the side, out of the way to keep traffic flowing. Of course there was nothing to see on-site. However, he had to admire the choice of location for a kidnapping.

The traffic at the time had been heavy and with steadily

moving vehicles. The kidnapping occurred in broad daylight, and the shift happened fast enough that no one understood. There'd been enough room for the vehicles behind to drive around, and that had kept many from stopping to inform the authorities that something was amiss—at least amiss enough to contact law enforcement and not just the port authorities.

Several of the surrounding vehicles' license plates had been caught on cameras, and the owners had been telephoned to see if they'd seen anything.

It wasn't a big surprise that most hadn't seen anything, other than a few people walking around a vehicle that had obviously broken down. As the traffic had been heavy, most of the drivers had been focused on getting to the next part of their journey, rather than watching what anyone else was doing.

The port itself was huge and incredibly efficient, as they moved thousands of people back and forth. A broken-down vehicle was towed out of the way and dealt with using the same efficiency. Only after several hours did anyone understand that the vehicle was more important than anyone had thought.

Of course all intel was out of Radar's reach, although he'd texted Terk several times, sending bits of information he'd gathered on the issue.

Hell, by rights, Radar shouldn't even be here. He'd just come from helping Bullard out on several jobs, when Levi had suggested that Radar travel to England to meet Terk.

"He, they, are your kind of people," Levi had said.

"What the hell does that mean?" Radar had asked in surprise. "Since when do I have a 'kind of people.'"

Levi's gaze never wavered, and something was eerie

about that long straight-on look from such steady eyes. "We all have a 'kind' of people. And I guarantee that Terk is yours."

"And you aren't?"

Levi's grin flashed—even matched the flash in his gaze. "Absolutely. Terk is our kind of people too, yet in a different manner."

The way he had said it made Radar back off slightly. He'd spent a lifetime being … different. And he wasn't, as far as he could see. Yet he'd always felt it. Like he was *faking it until he made it* type of thing. Joining the military had changed all that, but, every once in a while, it still reared its ugly head. Like now.

Who the hell was this Terk guy anyway?

So far, wandering around Calais, waiting for the rest of this hastily put together team to pick him up, he could only wonder what he'd gotten himself into.

JUST AS GAGE took a seat on a small local flight, he texted Terk. **Things to put on the damn list: airplane, airport, helicopter, helipad.**

He settled back and buckled in, wondering what the hell this trip would be all about. His phone buzzed, as the file from Jonas finally downloaded. Time was beyond being of the essence at this point, but, as he read Terk's incoming message, he learned that Radar was apparently already on the other side of the tunnel, checking out the area. He was tasked with checking for possibilities and looking to see if anybody could have gotten off and escaped. He was also questioning staff, and meanwhile the team was looking at tech options, hacking into the tunnel cameras, and all that online sleuthing.

Terk was apparently still waiting for formal permission from Jonas for that.

Gage just snorted and settled back, staring out the window. This would be one of those times when permission would be a foregone decision; otherwise the work would never get done. The fact that they had very little information on where these people went missing was already a problem. What happened to the men who had been on the assignment? Had they come back, or had they gone missing too? Way too much had been left unsaid, and that raised a whole different question. Had they been bribed or had they been taken out? Gage hoped it was bribed. *Taken out* was all too common in scenarios like this, but one could only hope not.

The flight was short, which was a good thing. Gage had just enough time to go through the little bits of information and to write up a list of questions. He fired the questions off to Terk, not knowing if they should go directly to Jonas or not but figured that maybe, for the moment, it would be better to go Terk's way. Later, if Gage didn't get answers fast enough, he'd be on Jonas's case pretty damn quick. As far as Gage figured, he had about thirty minutes, and then he'd blow up MI6's phone.

When Gage finally got off his flight, he looked around the airport, grabbed the rental vehicle that Tasha had arranged, and headed for the tunnel.

Flying to this side of the tunnel was faster and would save him some time, compared to going over on the ferry, but he still needed to know if somebody was on this side and if they had already done some work. After setting up his cell phone on his dashboard, he phoned Terk. "I picked up the rental, and I'm inching my way toward the entrance to the tunnel. What's the status?"

"Riff has agreed to help, and he's currently on your side of the tunnel."

"Well," he said in surprise, "that sounds good. Any chance he's done any reconnaissance yet?"

"I gave him your license plate number, so keep your door unlocked, and I suspect he'll join you in a few minutes."

"Good thing you warned me. So, you've got Radar on the other side. Correct?"

"Yes, apparently."

Since Radar and Riff were both people Gage had yet to work with, he felt his own guards coming up. Yet he left just enough for a probe. As much as he would like to think he was back to full strength, he couldn't help but reserve some of his strength in order to keep Lorelei safe back at Guardian central. He smirked at that. "Really, the Guardians?" he asked out loud.

He pulled into his lane, inching forward at a crawl. Just then the passenger door opened, and he turned to watch as a stranger, six-foot-four, heavily muscled, sat down in the truck beside him. Gage gave him a hard look, then turned back to face the windshield. "Hello, Riff. I'm Gage."

Riff gave a quick nod and didn't say anything.

"Get a chance to do any reconnaissance?"

Riff again nodded. "Yeah, though nothing to see. If anybody left from here, there aren't any tracks. We don't have any access to the tunnel computers yet."

"Yeah, we'll have to get Tasha and Sophia on that."

At that, Riff turned to look at him. "They'll have to hack into it."

"Maybe, maybe not," he muttered. He quickly hit Dial on Terk's number, and when Terk answered, Gage said, "Riff is here beside me. Nothing to see or hear at this point."

At that, Riff leaned forward to the phone. "Terk." It seemed more of an acknowledgment than anything else.

With a smile in his voice, Terk said, "Hey, Riff. Good to hear your voice."

"Says you," he said comfortably. "I don't have means to hack into the computers here."

"No, we're giving MI6 another ten minutes to give us formal permission. Then, after that, we'll do it on our own."

At that, Riff looked over at Gage and asked, "Do you have the facilities to do the hacking?"

"Yep," Terk replied.

Gage gave Riff a feral grin. "Facilities and personnel both."

Riff's eyebrows shot up, and then he gave an approving nod. "Good thing. I'm hoping for a fast job myself."

"Did you get any line on what happened to your fiancée?" Terk asked.

Riff's shoulders stiffened. Then he settled against the passenger seat. "I got a name."

"Give me the name," Terk said immediately. Riff hesitated. "Come on, Riff. We can do all the background and pull information you may not have been able to access yet," Terk said. "That'll take some time. So, while you're doing that, we can help you out with this."

"His name's Argyle, Argyle McNamara."

"Okay, and we'll need some information about where she was killed, what she was doing, that sort of thing. Just give me anything you can think of, relevant or not."

"I already emailed you the file," he stated solemnly.

"You've got from now to when we wrap up this job to get as much information as you can."

"Then what?" Gage asked, as he pulled the truck forward and started into the entrance of the tunnel itself.

"Then I'm off on my own."

"Some of these jobs are easier to do when you've got some backup," Gage noted, keeping his tone mild. He could sense the anger and frustration radiating off the silent man at his side. But that strong wall surrounding the man interested Gage the most. They hadn't had a chance to even ask Terk what Riff's abilities were, and, from just looking at him, it wasn't anything Gage could see, but the man had a shield like he'd never seen before. He sent Terk a communique telepathically. *What are Riff's abilities?*

The response came back a little garbled. *They're changing on him. He's so full of anger and frustration that I'm worried about what happens afterward.*

Great, so you sent me out with somebody who's a ticking bomb. Gage snorted. *Like I need that shit.*

Oh, I don't think he is a danger to you or any of us, Terk replied immediately. *However, when he finds whoever it is who killed his fiancée …*

Got it. Giving a slight headshake, Gage stared out, as he proceeded through the tunnel, sitting in the vehicle, just waiting to move on through.

"Terk, did you find out what happened? Do we have any intel?" Riff asked hurriedly.

"Give me your email, and I'll send you the file. We don't have much." Without waiting for the email to reach Riff, Terk gave him the verbal rundown. "Apparently MI6 did a silent catch-and-retrieve and were coming over on the ferry but somehow lost track of both their two prisoners and their own guys, somewhere between the two sides."

"This isn't exactly an easy place to kidnap anybody."

"No, it's not. I suspect that they lost them on the other side and either were given decoys or were taken out before they got very far."

"The intel seems pretty sparse."

"Yeah, one of those secret under-the-radar missions, and, on top of that, everybody disappeared."

"So … just *poof*? And nobody knows what the hell happened?"

"Exactly. No one. All they had was confirmation of the catch."

Riff didn't say anything, but he settled back again and studied his phone, as the information came in. He shook his head. "Is MI6 still as useless as ever?"

Gage cracked a smile. "Well, I'm pretty sure they would hate to hear my answer, but, in many ways, I would say yes. We have one person there who we work with exclusively."

Riff laughed. "Don't tell me. … Jonas."

At that, Gage looked at him and then slowly nodded. "Yes, Jonas."

Riff nodded. "Jonas is a square shooter at least. I dealt with him once, and he was okay."

"What did you do before this?"

"I worked for a private security firm … in France."

At that, Gage stiffened and glared at him. "Did you have anything to do with that mess with Bullard?"

"No, I had actually moved on, before Bullard came in and blew everything up. It was for the better though. Things were getting pretty ugly. There's quite a bit more work to be done to straighten things up over there."

"I hear you," Gage agreed, swearing as he thought about it. "We had a hell of a time getting Bullard back home."

"The fact that you even found him and got him back

again is pretty amazing—not to mention that most of the core team survived it all. Those guys don't fool around."

"None of us do," he confirmed.

Riff turned and looked at him, his eyes blazing an almost golden color. "Look. I've personally known Terk for years," he said, "and we've known of each other for far longer than that, but I don't know you at all."

Gage felt something inside Riff teeming with temper, and Gage nodded. "You will after this."

Find Radar here!

To find out more visit Dale Mayer's website.

geni.us/DMRadarUniversal

Magnus: Shadow Recon (Book #1)

Deep in the permafrost of the Arctic, a joint task force, comprised of over one dozen countries, comes together to level up their winter skills. A mix of personalities, nationalities, and egos bring out the best—and the worst—as these globally elite men and women work and play together. They rub elbows with hardy locals and a group of scientists gathered close by …

One fatality is almost expected with this training. A second is tough but not a surprise. However, when a third goes missing? It's hard to not be suspicious. When the missing man is connected to one of the elite Maverick team members and is a special friend of Lieutenant Commander Mason Callister? All hell breaks loose …

LIEUTENANT COMMANDER MASON Callister walked into the private office and stood in front of retired Navy Commander Doran Magellan.

"Mason, good to see you."

Yet the dry tone of voice, and the scowl pinching the silver-haired man, all belied his words. Mason had known Doran for over a decade, and their friendship had only grown over time.

Mason waited, as he watched the other man try to work the new tech phone system on his desk. With his hand circling the air above the black box, he appeared to hit buttons randomly.

Mason held back his amusement but to no avail.

"Why can't a phone be a phone anymore?" the commander snapped, as his glare shifted from Mason to the box and back.

Asking the commander if he needed help wouldn't make the older man feel any better, but sitting here and watching as he indiscriminately punched buttons was a struggle. "Is Helen away?" Mason asked.

"Yes, damn it. She's at lunch, and I need her to be at lunch." The commander's piercing gaze pinned Mason in place. "No one is to know you're here."

Solemn, Mason nodded. "Understood."

"Doran? Is that you?" A crotchety voice slammed into the room through the phone's speakers. "Get away from that damn phone. You keep clicking buttons in my ear. Get

Helen in there to do this."

"No, she can't be here for this."

Silence came first, then a huge groan. "Damn it. Then you should have connected me last, so I don't have to sit here and listen to you fumbling around."

"Go pour yourself a damn drink then," Doran barked. "I'm working on the others."

A snort was his only response.

Mason bit the inside of his lip, as he really tried to hold back his grin. The retired commander had been hell on wheels while on active duty, and, even now, the retired part of his life seemed to be more of a euphemism than anything.

"Damn things ..."

Mason looked around the dark mahogany office and the walls filled with photos, awards, medals. A life of purpose, accomplishment. And all of that had only piqued his interest during the initial call he'd received, telling him to be here at this time.

"Ah, got it."

Mason's eyebrows barely twitched, as the commander gave him a feral grin. "I'd rather lead a warship into battle than deal with some of today's technology."

As he was one of only a few commanders who'd been in a position to do such a thing, it said much about his capabilities.

And much about current technology.

The commander leaned back in his massive chair and motioned to the cart beside Mason. "Pour three cups."

Interesting. Mason walked a couple steps across the rich tapestry-style carpet and lifted the silver service to pour coffee into three very down-to-earth-looking mugs.

"Black for me."

Mason picked up two cups and walked one over to Doran.

"Thanks." He leaned forward and snapped into the phone, "Everyone here?"

Multiple voices responded.

Curiouser and curiouser. Mason recognized several of the voices. Other relics of an era gone by. Although not a one would like to hear that, and, in good faith, it wasn't fair. Mason had thought each of these men were retired, had relinquished power. Yet, as he studied Doran in front of him, Mason had to wonder if any of them actually had passed the baton or if they'd only slid into the shadows. Was this planned with the government's authority? Or were these retirees a shadow group to the government?

The tangible sense of power and control oozed from Doran's words, tone, stature—his very pores. This man might be heading into his sunset years—based on a simple calculation of chronological years spent on the planet—but he was a long way from being out of the action.

"Mason ..." Doran began.

"Sir?"

"We've got a problem."

Mason narrowed his gaze and waited.

Doran's glare was hard, steely hard, with an icy glint. "Do you know the Mavericks?"

Mason's eyebrows shot up. The black ops division was one of those well-kept secrets, so, therefore, everyone knew about it. He gave a decisive nod. "I do."

"And you're involved in the logistics behind the ICE training program in the Arctic, are you not?"

"I am." Now where was the commander going with this?

"Do you know another SEAL by the name of Mountain

193

Rode? He's been working for the black ops Mavericks." At his own words, the commander shook his head. "What the hell was his mother thinking when she gave him that moniker?"

"She wasn't thinking anything," said the man with a hard voice from behind Mason.

He stiffened slightly, then relaxed as he recognized that voice too.

"She died giving birth to me. And my full legal name is Mountain Bear Rode. It was my father's doing."

The commander glared at the new arrival. "Did I say you could come in?"

"Yes." Mountain's voice was firm, yet a definitive note of affection filled his tone.

That emotion told Mason so much.

The commander harrumphed, then cleared his throat. "Mason, we're picking up a significant amount of chatter over that ICE training. Most of it good. Some of it the usual caterwauling we've come to expect every time we participate in a joint training mission. This one is set to run for six months, then to reassess."

Mason already knew this. But he waited for the commander to get around to why Mason was here, and, more important, what any of this had to do with the mountain of a man who now towered beside him.

The commander shifted his gaze to Mountain, but he remained silent.

Mason noted Mountain was not only physically big but damn imposing and severely pissed, seemingly barely holding back the forces within. His body language seemed to yell, *And the world will fix this, or I'll find the reason why.*

For a moment Mason felt sorry for the world.

Finally a voice spoke through the phone. "Mason, this is

Alpha here. I run the Mavericks. We've got a problem with that ICE training center. Mountain, tell him."

Mason shifted to include Mountain in his field of vision. Mason wished the other men on the conference call were in the room too. It was one thing to deal with men you knew and could take the measure of; it was another when they were silent shadows in the background.

"My brother is one of the men who reported for the Artic training three weeks ago."

"Tergan Rode?" Mason confirmed. "I'm the one who arranged for him to go up there. He's a great kid."

A glimmer of a smile cracked Mountain's stony features. He nodded. "Indeed. A bright light in my often dark world. He's a dozen years younger than me, just passed his BUD/s training this spring, and raring to go. Until his raring to go then got up and went."

Oh, shit. Mason's gaze zinged to the commander, who had kicked up his feet to rest atop the big desk. Stocking feet. With Mickey Mouse images dancing on them. Sidetracked, Mason struggled to pull his attention back to Mountain. "Meaning?"

"He's disappeared." Mountain let out a harsh breath, as if just saying that out loud, and maybe to the right people, could allow him to relax—at least a little.

The commander spoke up. "We need your help, Mason. You're uniquely qualified for this problem."

It didn't sound like he was qualified in any way for anything he'd heard so far. "Clarify." His spoken word was simplicity itself, but the tone behind it said he wanted the cards on the table ... now.

Mountain spoke up. "He's the third incident."

Mason's gaze narrowed, as the reports from the training camp rolled through his mind. "One was Russian. One was from the German SEAL team. Both were deemed accidental deaths."

"No, they weren't."

There it was. The root of the problem in black-and-white. He studied Mountain, aiming for neutrality. "Do you have evidence?"

"My brother did."

"Ah, hell."

Mountain gave a clipped nod. "I'm going to find him."

"Of that I have no doubt," Mason said quietly. "Do you have a copy of the evidence he collected?"

"I have some of it." Mountain held out a USB key. "This is your copy. Top secret."

"We don't have to remind you, Mason, that lives are at stake," Doran added. "Nor do we need another international incident. Consider also that a group of scientists, studying global warming, is close by, and not too far away is a village home to a few hardy locals."

Mason accepted the key, turned to the commander, and asked, "Do we know if this is internal or enemy warfare?"

"We don't know at this point," Alpha replied through the phone. "Mountain will lead Shadow Recon. His mission is twofold. One, find out what's behind these so-called accidents and put a stop to it by any means necessary. Two, locate his brother, hopefully alive."

"And where do I come in?" Mason asked.

"We want you to pull together a special team. The members of Shadow Recon will report to both you and Mountain, just in case."

That was clear enough.

"You'll stay stateside but in constant communication with Mountain—with the caveat that, if necessary, you're on the next flight out."

"What about bringing in other members from the Mavericks?" Mason suggested.

Alpha took this question too, his response coming through via Speakerphone. "We don't have the numbers. The budget for our division has been cut. So we called the commander to pull some strings."

That was Doran's cue to explain further. "Mountain has fought hard to get me on board with this plan, and I'm here now. The navy has a special budget for Shadow Recon and will take care of Mountain and you, Mason, and the team you provide."

"Skills needed?"

"Everything," Mountain said, his voice harsh. "But the biggest is these men need to operate in the shadows, mostly alone, without a team beside them. Too many new arrivals will alert the enemy. If we make any changes to the training program, it will raise alarms. We'll move the men in one or two at a time on the same rotation that the trainees are running right now."

"And when we get to the bottom of this?" Mason looked from the commander back to Mountain.

"Then the training can resume as usual," Doran stated.

Mason immediately churned through the names already popping up in his mind. How much could he tell his men? Obviously not much. Hell, he didn't know much himself. How much time did he have? "Timeline?"

The commander's final word told him of the urgency.

"Yesterday."

Find Magnus here!

To find out more visit Dale Mayer's website.

https://geni.us/DMSRMagnusUniversal

Author's Note

Thank you for reading Terkel's Triumph: Terkel's Team, Book 9! If you enjoyed the book, please take a moment and leave a short review.

Dear reader,

I love to hear from readers, and you can contact me at my website: www.dalemayer.com or at my Facebook author page. To be informed of new releases and special offers, sign up for my newsletter or follow me on BookBub. And if you are interested in joining Dale Mayer's Reader Group, here is the Facebook sign up page.
http://geni.us/DaleMayerFBGroup

Cheers,
Dale Mayer

Get THREE Free Books Now!

Have you met the SEALS of Honor?

SEALs of Honor Books 1, 2, and 3. Follow the stories of brave, badass warriors who serve their country with honor and love their women to the limits of life and death.

Read Mason, Hawk, and Dane right now for FREE.

Go here and tell me where to send them!
https://dalemayer.com/masonfree

About the Author

Dale Mayer is a *USA Today* best-selling author, best known for her SEALs military romances, her Psychic Visions series, and her Lovely Lethal Garden cozy series. Her contemporary romances are raw and full of passion and emotion (Broken But … Mending, Hathaway House series). Her thrillers will keep you guessing (Kate Morgan, By Death series), and her romantic comedies will keep you giggling (*It's a Dog's Life*, a stand-alone novella; and the Broken Protocols series, starring Charming Marvin, the cat).

Dale honors the stories that come to her—and some of them are crazy, break all the rules and cross multiple genres!

To go with her fiction, she also writes nonfiction in many different fields, with books available on résumé writing, companion gardening, and the US mortgage system. All her books are available in print and ebook format.

Connect with Dale Mayer Online

Dale's Website – www.dalemayer.com
Twitter – @DaleMayer
Facebook Page – geni.us/DaleMayerFBFanPage
Facebook Group – geni.us/DaleMayerFBGroup
BookBub – geni.us/DaleMayerBookbub
Instagram – geni.us/DaleMayerInstagram
Goodreads – geni.us/DaleMayerGoodreads
Newsletter – geni.us/DaleNews

Also by Dale Mayer

Published Adult Books:

Shadow Recon
Magnus, Book 1

Bullard's Battle
Ryland's Reach, Book 1
Cain's Cross, Book 2
Eton's Escape, Book 3
Garret's Gambit, Book 4
Kano's Keep, Book 5
Fallon's Flaw, Book 6
Quinn's Quest, Book 7
Bullard's Beauty, Book 8
Bullard's Best, Book 9
Bullard's Battle, Books 1–2
Bullard's Battle, Books 3–4
Bullard's Battle, Books 5–6
Bullard's Battle, Books 7–8

Terkel's Team
Damon's Deal, Book 1
Wade's War, Book 2
Gage's Goal, Book 3
Calum's Contact, Book 4
Rick's Road, Book 5

Scott's Summit, Book 6
Brody's Beast, Book 7
Terkel's Twist, Book 8
Terkel's Triumph, Book 9

Terkel's Guardian
Radar, Book 1

Kate Morgan
Simon Says... Hide, Book 1
Simon Says... Jump, Book 2
Simon Says... Ride, Book 3
Simon Says... Scream, Book 4
Simon Says... Run, Book 5
Simon Says... Walk, Book 6

Hathaway House
Aaron, Book 1
Brock, Book 2
Cole, Book 3
Denton, Book 4
Elliot, Book 5
Finn, Book 6
Gregory, Book 7
Heath, Book 8
Iain, Book 9
Jaden, Book 10
Keith, Book 11
Lance, Book 12
Melissa, Book 13
Nash, Book 14
Owen, Book 15

The K9 Files

The K9 Files, Books 9–10
The K9 Files, Books 11–12

Lovely Lethal Gardens

Arsenic in the Azaleas, Book 1
Bones in the Begonias, Book 2
Corpse in the Carnations, Book 3
Daggers in the Dahlias, Book 4
Evidence in the Echinacea, Book 5
Footprints in the Ferns, Book 6
Gun in the Gardenias, Book 7
Handcuffs in the Heather, Book 8
Ice Pick in the Ivy, Book 9
Jewels in the Juniper, Book 10
Killer in the Kiwis, Book 11
Lifeless in the Lilies, Book 12
Murder in the Marigolds, Book 13
Nabbed in the Nasturtiums, Book 14
Offed in the Orchids, Book 15
Poison in the Pansies, Book 16
Quarry in the Quince, Book 17
Revenge in the Roses, Book 18
Silenced in the Sunflowers, Book 19
Toes in the Tulips, Book 20
Lovely Lethal Gardens, Books 1–2
Lovely Lethal Gardens, Books 3–4
Lovely Lethal Gardens, Books 5–6
Lovely Lethal Gardens, Books 7–8
Lovely Lethal Gardens, Books 9–10

Psychic Vision Series

Tuesday's Child

Hide 'n Go Seek
Maddy's Floor
Garden of Sorrow
Knock Knock…
Rare Find
Eyes to the Soul
Now You See Her
Shattered
Into the Abyss
Seeds of Malice
Eye of the Falcon
Itsy-Bitsy Spider
Unmasked
Deep Beneath
From the Ashes
Stroke of Death
Ice Maiden
Snap, Crackle…
What If…
Talking Bones
String of Tears
Psychic Visions Books 1–3
Psychic Visions Books 4–6
Psychic Visions Books 7–9

By Death Series
Touched by Death
Haunted by Death
Chilled by Death
By Death Books 1–3

Broken Protocols – Romantic Comedy Series
Cat's Meow
Cat's Pajamas
Cat's Cradle
Cat's Claus
Broken Protocols 1-4

Broken and... Mending
Skin
Scars
Scales (of Justice)
Broken but... Mending 1-3

Glory
Genesis
Tori
Celeste
Glory Trilogy

Biker Blues
Morgan: Biker Blues, Volume 1
Cash: Biker Blues, Volume 2

SEALs of Honor
Mason: SEALs of Honor, Book 1
Hawk: SEALs of Honor, Book 2
Dane: SEALs of Honor, Book 3
Swede: SEALs of Honor, Book 4
Shadow: SEALs of Honor, Book 5
Cooper: SEALs of Honor, Book 6
Markus: SEALs of Honor, Book 7
Evan: SEALs of Honor, Book 8

Heroes for Hire

Heroes for Hire, Books 10–12
Heroes for Hire, Books 13–15
Heroes for Hire, Books 16–18
Heroes for Hire, Books 19–21
Heroes for Hire, Books 22–24

SEALs of Steel

Badger: SEALs of Steel, Book 1
Erick: SEALs of Steel, Book 2
Cade: SEALs of Steel, Book 3
Talon: SEALs of Steel, Book 4
Laszlo: SEALs of Steel, Book 5
Geir: SEALs of Steel, Book 6
Jager: SEALs of Steel, Book 7
The Final Reveal: SEALs of Steel, Book 8
SEALs of Steel, Books 1–4
SEALs of Steel, Books 5–8
SEALs of Steel, Books 1–8

The Mavericks

Kerrick, Book 1
Griffin, Book 2
Jax, Book 3
Beau, Book 4
Asher, Book 5
Ryker, Book 6
Miles, Book 7
Nico, Book 8
Keane, Book 9
Lennox, Book 10
Gavin, Book 11
Shane, Book 12

Diesel, Book 13

Jerricho, Book 14

Killian, Book 15

Hatch, Book 16

Corbin, Book 17

Aiden, Book 18

The Mavericks, Books 1–2

The Mavericks, Books 3–4

The Mavericks, Books 5–6

The Mavericks, Books 7–8

The Mavericks, Books 9–10

The Mavericks, Books 11–12

Collections
Dare to Be You…

Dare to Love…

Dare to be Strong…

RomanceX3

Standalone Novellas
It's a Dog's Life

Riana's Revenge

Second Chances

Published Young Adult Books:

Family Blood Ties Series
Vampire in Denial

Vampire in Distress

Vampire in Design

Vampire in Deceit

Vampire in Defiance

Vampire in Conflict

Vampire in Chaos

Vampire in Crisis

Vampire in Control

Vampire in Charge

Family Blood Ties Set 1–3

Family Blood Ties Set 1–5

Family Blood Ties Set 4–6

Family Blood Ties Set 7–9

Sian's Solution, A Family Blood Ties Series Prequel
Novelette

Design series

Dangerous Designs

Deadly Designs

Darkest Designs

Design Series Trilogy

Standalone

In Cassie's Corner

Gem Stone (a Gemma Stone Mystery)

Time Thieves

Published Non-Fiction Books:

Career Essentials

Career Essentials: The Résumé

Career Essentials: The Cover Letter

Career Essentials: The Interview

Career Essentials: 3 in 1

Made in United States
North Haven, CT
02 April 2023